T0271559

DARKOME

DARKOME

HANNU RAJANIEMI

First published in Great Britain in 2024 by Gollancz
an imprint of The Orion Publishing Group Ltd
Carmelite House, 50 Victoria Embankment
London EC4Y 0DZ

An Hachette UK Company

The authorised representative in the EEA is Hachette Ireland,
8 Castlecourt Centre, Dublin 15, D15 XTP3, Ireland (email: info@hbgi.ie)

3 5 7 9 10 8 6 4

A CIP catalogue record for this book
is available from the British Library.

ISBN (Trade Paperback) 978 1 473 20332 7
ISBN (eBook) 978 1 473 20334 1

Typeset by Deltatype Ltd, Birkenhead, Merseyside
Printed in Great Britain by Clays Ltd, Elcograph S.p.A

www.gollancz.co.uk

To the biocurious.

Biology is a study, not in being, but in becoming.

— Carl Woese & Nigel Goldenfeld

Prologue
Black Rock City, 2042

You found this message in a DNA sample. I don't know exactly where you got it from. Perhaps you dabbed a touchscreen with a silicon toothpick, or received a postcard with a tiny stain inside the letter 'o'. Somebody shook your hand, or kissed you, or left a used condom on your doorstep. Darkome is everywhere, in all the hidden places where the darksense takes you.

You fed your sample into a DNA sequencer, and out came a long string of As and Ts and Gs and Cs. The app in your Eyes decrypted it and turned it into conversation threads and tokens, into a library of genetic parts for growing almost anything – for turning *you* into almost anything. You scrolled through the HOWTOs, imagining what you could do. Make bioluminescent ink for a glowing tattoo. Grow a steak to feed your hungry child. Release carbon-capturing cyanobacteria to save the planet.

And then the title of this post caught your eye.

HOW TO SAVE DARKOME.

I know, I know: all those other things sound much cooler than a manifesto. But writing this is the last thing I'll ever do, so please try to make it to the end.

Don't worry, it's not going to be very long. I don't have much time left. The Heffalump has built a dark palace in my body, and all the things I have tried, neoantigen vaccines and CAR-NKs and cytotoxic proteins and dimeric kill switches with DNA binders for specific mutations, are not doing much. I'm shaking with fever from the cytokine storm and have a blinding headache. The Heffalump is not going anywhere. I have merely pushed her to evolve.

But I'm going to keep talking, dictating this to Donnie the AI, letting it fill in the details. And if I'm done before the final dark, I'm going to go out and dance until sunrise.

Don't waste any pity on me, though. They are going to come after you now, because of what I did. And the only way I can help is by telling you what I've learned.

How not to cure your cancer.

How not to pack for Burning Man.

How not to fuck up life itself.

I need you to know these things. And once you do, I need you to be like the Heffalump. Take everything they throw at you, and use it to get better at surviving. If you make it, if you learn from my mistakes, one day people will see that you are not the cancer: it's the old, broken world around you that is the disease, and you are the cure.

And maybe you will make it, and a million years from now, you will be a star-spore riding a laser beam, with all of Darkome in your genome, and this tiny part of me will be with you for ever.

That thought makes me smile. But right now, I am a stranger, dying in the desert. And before we can go to the stars, I have to tell you how I got here.

Part One

The Harbour, 2039

1

The Aspis

It began with cells and DNA, like life always does.

The cells were Mom's, a layer of liquid in ninety-six tiny wells on a plastic plate, inside the makeshift cell culture hood in our houseboat *Maré Viva*'s lab. They had already outlived her by two months. They came from her kidney tumour and were practically immortal. If I wanted, I could keep a part of her alive for ever.

Instead, I was trying to kill them, to figure out what had killed her.

I pushed my gloved hands through the hood's vinyl curtain and started dosing the wells with my sixteen-channel Eppendorf pipette. It was a birthday present from Mom, a channel for each year. I had been so proud. She thought I was ready. 'We are a team now, peixinha,' she said, using my family nickname, 'little fish' in Portuguese. I hugged her hard, and she gave me one of her bright smiles. 'Cancer might as well give up and grow potatoes in China.'

My eyes stung, but I had no time for tears. This was the key part of the experiment. A twitch of my hand would waste almost two weeks of work. I focused on the hum of the hood's HEPA unit and pressed the pipette's contoured trigger. Sixteen teardrops of mRNA fell onto Mom in sixteen wells. I moved the pipette, pressed, moved and pressed, six times in all.

Then it was done. I blew out the long breath I had been holding in. Mom's cells now had chemical instructions to make a key piece they were missing, a protein called p53. It guards our DNA from damage and kills mutated cells – like cancer.

Like Mom and other females in my extended family, I have Li-Fraumeni syndrome, a genetic disease. Our cells don't know how to make p53 on their own, so we are tumour hotbeds. By age seventeen I had already fought cancer twice, and had the scars to show for it. There was no cure. Li-Fraumeni was too rare for big pharma to bother with. Mom and I were doomed to play whack-a-mole with every known cancer type for the rest of our lives.

Two years ago, Mom had brought us to the Harbour to change that. But somehow, somewhere, we had made a mistake, and she had paid the price. And if I couldn't figure out what had gone wrong, sooner or later I would pay it too.

I closed the hood, ejected the pipette heads into the consumables basket and put the Eppendorf back into its rack on the long stainless steel bench. I would check in on the cells with a microscope in a few hours. I was looking for cells that *weren't* dying, for mRNA that wasn't doing its job. I had spent the last two weeks making p53 mRNA over and over, varying the reaction parameters ever so slightly. My latest theory was that the issue was the RNA itself. In certain conditions, the enzymes we used to make it could become error-prone. Mom's cells might have ended up making a kind of anti-p53 that shut down whatever she had left naturally – and supercharged her brain tumour.

My macule itched. The giant birthmark on my forehead was the only visible sign of my condition. Mom always said it looked like Superman's shield. I peeled my lab gloves off and scratched it. I squirmed out from the lab corner's maze of instruments, walked barefoot across the patchwork of old rugs and flopped on my back on the small couch with the hand-embroidered pillows. The porthole window above showed a patch of indigo sky.

I took out my Eyes, folded into handheld phone mode, and checked the time. It was almost six in the evening. I wouldn't have anything resembling results before midnight. It would have been sensible to get some sleep, but I had taken a large modafinil dose around noon and the stimulant gave everything a tingly, nervous clarity. I decided to design the next experiment while this one was running. That was one of Mallory's principles. The grand old dame of the Harbour's biohackers had instilled in us the idea that you always did the next obvious thing *now*. Biology was unpredictable and the first thing was unlikely to work, so you had to hedge your bets. Of course, I was into my seventh or eighth thing now, but the principle still applied.

Besides, the work anchored me against the pull of the dark whirlpool in my chest.

I stared at the bundles of old herbs and dried seaweed hanging from the ceiling beams and tried to gather my thoughts. 'Open lab notebook,' I told my Eyes. But before I got any further, the door opened, and Dad walked in.

'Hi, Inara,' he said.

His round face looked haggard and his greying beard was

unkempt. I hadn't seen him for a couple of days. The N95 respirator marks on his cheeks suggested he had been in the default world, away from the Harbour. He carried a slim white bag that could have been from the Apple Store. Was he trying to mend fences with a gift he couldn't afford? The new Eyes 7 model that had just launched at the WWDC?

He lumbered over and sat on the edge of the couch. I sat up, cross-legged, and folded my arms.

'What's up?' I asked warily.

A month ago, I had been out with my boyfriend Jerome, at a beach rave by the Good Hot saunas in Point Molate. We had stayed out until 3 a.m. Jerome had all but dragged me there, in a vain effort to cheer me up. I had nursed half a Corona for the whole night, crouching by the bonfire. While the music played, I stared into the flames and thought about mRNA.

When I came home, Dad exploded. He screamed at me at the top of his voice. He said I was thoughtless and disrespectful. I dishonoured Mom's memory. I should be ashamed. He looked ridiculous in his old umbrella-patterned pyjamas with his hairy belly peeking out, but rage poured out of him in waves. When I tried to go past him to my bunk, he took a sudden step towards me, like an animal about to attack. When I flinched, he started crying and collapsed on the bottom bed he had shared with Mom.

I spent the subsequent three nights in Jerome's AirStreamer until Holst talked to Dad and got him to take a sleeping pill. He was sheepish and apologetic afterwards. Holst said it was sleep deprivation, that it wasn't uncommon after bereavement. But it was like being bitten by a dog. You never looked at it the same way again.

'So,' he said. 'Uh.' He shifted in his seat, and the couch groaned. Folds of skin hung loose from his tattooed arms, but he was still a big man. He set the bag down between us. I reached for it, but he covered it with a beefy hand.

'I want you to listen to me before you open it.'

I nodded.

'Inara, I always believed your mom could do anything. Maybe it was not literally true. But no one, and certainly not me, could ever stop her from doing what she wanted to do.

'So when she wanted to come here, I supported her, even if I had doubts. And this' – he gestured at the lab equipment in the corner – 'was always something you two shared, like the ... condition. Something I was not a part of. Something I could not understand.'

He squeezed his hands into fists. 'Well, I've been trying to understand. I've been studying. I know a bit more now, and ... and I found something.'

He opened the bag and took out a small box. On the cover was a coppery symbol that looked like a Greek hoplite's shield. The logo of Aspis. The most powerful biotech company in the world.

'Aspis is running a trial called PROSPERITY-A,' he said. 'For high risk cancer patients. It's not Li-Fraumeni specifically, but close enough. It's ...' He looked up like an actor trying to remember his lines. 'It's a new version of the Aspis chip. It has an integrated DNA sequencer. It can detect pre-cancerous mutations in your blood, and make mRNA vaccines on the fly to target them. Dr Nguyen says it would be perfect for you. They ... they want you to enrol, Inara. You simply need to agree.' He smiled. 'Your mom believed in providence, Inara. I never did. Until now.'

9

I picked up the box and opened it. The Aspis lay in the padded nest inside. It was a white disc the size of a large wristwatch face, with a tiny touchscreen in the middle. Next to it, an adjustable mauve strap lay in its own compartment.

I picked it up. It was smooth metal, expensively heavy, definitely better build quality than the ubiquitous government-subsidised models. The underside had tiny Velcro-like burs – microneedles that would go through skin painlessly, sample blood and deliver mRNA into the dermis.

Aspis had single-handedly ended the Decade of Plagues with a wearable that made mRNA vaccines on demand. It made immunisations against a new virus as easy as rolling out a software patch. Now, hundreds of millions of people wore an Aspis around their upper arm. They were as common as Eyes, but in the Harbour and other Darkome communities like it, it was easy to forget they even existed. Here, in the aged wood interior of *Maré Viva*, next to our rough Plexiglass cell culture hood and ancient second-hand PCR machines, it seemed like an alien visitor from the future.

I felt a touch of awe. The disc in my hand was a miniature genomics lab and vaccine factory. It had more capabilities packed into it than all the equipment in the houseboat, maybe more than the Harbour's big community lab. Its microfluidic mRNA synthesiser could have done my two-week production run in minutes. Not only that, devices like it had saved civilisation, and were well on their way towards transforming medicine for ever.

All for a price, of course. Aspis was the antithesis of everything the Harbour and Darkome stood for. It didn't only detect pathogens. It spotted any foreign mRNA or DNA – anything biohackers like Mom and I made to change our biology ourselves – and flagged it up to the authorities. It was digital rights management for our bodies, and only Aspis had the keys.

'Dad. No. I can't.' I tossed the Aspis back into the box. 'Look.' I rubbed my forehead. 'I get it. You are trying to help. But you *know* I can't do this. The Harbour has one rule: no Aspises. Mallory will go ballistic the moment I turn this thing on. We would have to *leave*.'

He hunched down and rested his hands on his legs.

'Oh my God. That is what you *want*, isn't it?' I said. 'You never wanted to be here in the first place. And now you have an excuse to get out.'

'It's not an excuse, Inara. It's hope. This thing might save you. It might actually work, not like—' He paused.

'Not like whatever dangerous Darkome bullshit Mom and I spent the last two years on, is that what you are saying?'

The anger was a bright crack in my mind. Red light poured out. I held up the Aspis.

'Do you even realise what this thing does? It was one thing for the big tech to have control over our screens. But this actually plugs into our *bodies*. I'm not handing over keys to my immune system to some fucking tech bros. Mom wanted to be free from this bullshit, Dad. That's the whole *point* of Darkome.'

'I thought the point was for you and Manuela to get better,' Dad said quietly. 'She loved this community, that's true. She liked Holst and Mallory. Even Jerome. But Inara, coming here was always about *you*. Trust me, if there had been a better way, she would have taken it. Well, here it is.' He pointed at the Aspis. 'I get what you are saying. I worked for tech companies when I was younger. I know

11

how they think. But if it wasn't for Aspis – well, the world would be much worse off now.'

'Only because they crushed all the alternatives. Darkome vaccines work as well, you know that. I *am* going to figure this out, Dad. I'm so close.'

'That's what she always said.' Dad's voice broke. 'She was a terrible liar, too.'

'Fuck you, Dad. You didn't understand her. You never did. You are a pitiful little man who wants a pitiful little life.'

'And what's wrong with that?' he whispered.

'*Everything*.' Tears of anger flowed down my face. I stood up. 'If you want to leave, I'm not stopping you. But I'm staying here.'

'I don't want you to be afraid all the time. I don't want you to pour your life into – into all this in vain.' The shrill note I had heard that night after the bonfire crept into his voice. '*I* don't want to be afraid all the time. Inara, please.'

I took the Aspis. 'No. We're done. I'm going to throw this thing into the sea. Then I'm going to go back to work.'

He stood up and loomed over me.

'Inara. Don't.'

'What are you going to do? Kidnap me? You can't force me to join a clinical trial. California law. Want me to call child protection services?'

'You're right,' he said and adjusted his dark-rimmed glasses. His eyes were sad behind them. 'But ... I can make it harder for you to stay.'

'What do you mean?'

'Yesterday, I met with a journalist. They are very interested in a story about a woman who died from a DIY mRNA therapy, about a Darkome community where people are trying dangerous things.'

'That's not what happened and you *know* it. She already had a brain tumour. Maybe ... maybe there was a reaction, but she would have died *anyway*—'

'We don't know that,' Dad said sharply. 'I can go public with this, Inara. I can tell everyone what happened. What this place did to your mom. She deserves that. And no one else with your condition should go down this dangerous path.'

This couldn't be Dad. My Dad was afraid to jump a queue or negotiate rent. He was gentle. Everyone liked him. This wasn't even the hurting, angry animal Dad. This was someone else, cold and calculating.

And he wasn't bluffing. I saw it play out in my head. A big story about Mom and the Harbour would get global attention. California, especially the Bay Area, tended to turn a blind eye to Darkome communities, but there would be an investigation. A crackdown. Mallory for one, and Jerome, were involved in things that, while ethical, were definitely technically criminal.

Dad was talking about destroying the Harbour. Maybe all of Darkome.

'Seriously? You are blackmailing me?' My voice shook with disbelief.

'I don't want to do this, Inara. I care about this community too. But if we leave, you are free to join the trial. It's your choice.' His voice was strained.

'THAT'S NOT A FUCKING CHOICE,' I screamed. I threw the Aspis from me, as hard as I could. It flew across the room and hit something in our kitchenette with a pitiful metallic tinkle. The sound was not enough to quell my rage. My hands found a pillow from the couch. I pressed it to my face, bit down into the fabric hard and screamed until my breath gave out.

I let the pillow fall to the ground. 'That's not what freedom feels like,' I whispered. My throat hurt, another wave in an ocean of pain.

Dad extended a trembling hand, but I brushed it aside. Dark patches swam in my eyes. Somehow, I made it to the houseboat's door and outside, into the sea air.

2

The Dark Star

The sea was a darker brushstroke of blue beneath the sky. In the distance, clouds washed over San Francisco's skyline. It was the kind of evening that I would have normally spent sitting in the *Maré Viva*'s roof garden in a thick jacket, drinking cold brew coffee and designing experiments among tomato plants and herb pots.

But now I had to get away. I ran down the pier towards the shore, still barefoot. I didn't stop until I reached the sandy path on the beach. I leaned on my knees and gulped in air to fight nausea. The crisp air cleared my head, leaving one thought.

I had to tell Holst and Mallory.

The Harbour lay before me, cupped between the long wavebreaker on my left and the curve of the beach ahead. The lanterns strung between the two dozen houseboats and the community lab barge glowed with soft amber light. The Dark Star BBQ, a two-storey brick structure, loomed on the shore beyond the wall of boats. When it got darker, its circus-tent-like canopy would blaze with biolumin-escent dragons and piratical skulls. Its windows and the beer garden were already brightly lit. I could smell a hint of mammoth barbecue in the wind. It was a cappella night: everyone would be there.

I broke into a run on the soft sand. One of Darin's spider-goats lifted its head and gave me a suspicious look. I passed the giant bee statue that stood above the Harbour entrance like a tame kaiju. Here, the ground was too rough for bare-foot running, and I had to slow down. Up the brambly hillside, Holst's buckyball house glinted golden in a fading sunbeam. I knew the paths past it that led to hidden works of art. Juniper's living labyrinth; the quarry where you could drive tricycles that left bioluminescent trails at night like giant snails. Holst's grove where he pumped mRNA into the ground to talk to the mycelium.

Maybe it was the shock or the modafinil, but for a moment, it felt like my head was a snowglobe that contained this tiny realm that had adopted Mom and me. Dad was ready to shatter it — he had bought the shiny lie that Aspis was selling. I had to find a way to stop him.

I heard the choir before I entered the beer garden. The Conspiracy of Mustaches was in full swing with Leonard Cohen's 'Winter Lady'. Darin's baritone crooned the lyrics while Holst, Kieran and Z harmonised in the background. They infused the melancholy song with manic energy. The crowd clapped along and stomped their feet, sea shanty style.

I opened the skull-shaped gate and entered. The in vitro meat and hops smell from the main building was much stronger here. Most of the Harbour's two dozen permanent inhabitants huddled around the rough benches and tables. I scanned for Mallory – Holst, of course, was on the stage with the other performers, craggy horse-face half-hidden by an enormous fake Chevron handlebar. There was a brief hush when everyone registered my presence.

I blushed. I had spent the past two months mostly by myself, apart from receiving the occasional condolences, and the familiar faces around me felt like strangers. Lorena, who had been friends with Mom, lifted a ring-encrusted hand and waved me over. We had been trying to help her to make mRNA-encoded opsins for a brain–computer inter-face prototype. Like Mom's therapy, it had needed brain delivery. But I had no time for niceties. Dad might be giving me a bit of space, but sooner or later he would come looking for me, and I had to talk to the Harbour elders before he showed up.

I spotted Mallory and Jerome and made a beeline for them. They sat together at a table close to the stage. Jerome had already spotted me, got up and offered me a seat. I sat down gratefully.

Jerome had grown a thin beard since I'd last seen him, apparently in an attempt to hide the burn scar on his cheek. With his chiselled cheekbones and tousled hair, it made him look like a K-pop star cosplaying a pirate.

The sweat cooled on my skin, and I shivered. Mallory gave me a quizzical look, but Jerome took off his mushroom leather pilot jacket and draped it over me. 'Hey, Inara. It's good to see you.' I gave him a wan smile. 'Listen. You look like you could use a drink and some warm food. I'll be right back, OK?' He leaned closer. 'Let's catch up,' he whispered in my ear. 'It's been too long. And I have big news.'

I opened my mouth to sound the alarm, to tell him what had happened, but the Mustaches launched into another song, 'Suzanne' this time. By the time there was a gap in the music, Jerome was already headed for the Dark Star's kitchen.

Mallory watched him go. Her wrinkled face was framed by silver pixie hair, and her tiny body almost disappeared inside a long black leather coat. Her neck was covered in faded tattoos.

'Romeo has been moping,' she said. 'If you're back, please don't break him. He's handy in the lab.'

I raised my eyebrows. That was high praise coming from Mallory. She was a Harbour legend, the second person to settle here after Holst, and no one really knew her origin story. There were whispers she used to work for the NSA. Another rumour claimed she was actually Satoshi Nakamoto. Whatever the truth, she was almost certainly one of the chief architects of Darkome.

She had also been the only one to vote against Mom, me and Dad joining the Harbour.

Mallory stared at me with quiet intensity. I swallowed.

'Actually ... I wanted to talk to you about something.'

'Office hours are on Tuesdays. I'm here for the beer. Can it wait?' She lifted her thick-rimmed jailbroken Eyes and squinted. 'Shit, kid. You look like hell. What is it?'

I hesitated. Mallory would go apeshit if I told her the full truth. She had doxxed an anti-Darkome congressman for doing much less than what Dad was proposing to do. I had to play this carefully.

'Since, you know ... Mom, I have been thinking,' I said. 'What if there was an anti-Darkome crackdown? What if there was some high-profile incident that made the Feds come after us?'

18

Mallory perked up. 'It's a good question,' she said. 'I've been wargaming it with some devs. I have been telling Holst for years that the basic Darkome protocol is too open to be secure. It could really use a full rewrite. It's a historical accident, you know.' She gestured at the space around us. 'When the Plagues hit, we needed a DIY vaccine distribution platform ASAP. So we took on the technical debt. Mashed up Russian silkroad code with DNA. Sprinkled some El Paquete Semanal on top. Ugly as sin, but it worked.

'So yeah. We could do a lot better if push came to shove. We could go fully underground. Darkome would survive. But this place ...' Her face darkened. 'Well, they would have to pry my pipette from my cold dead hand.'

My heart fell. I had hoped Mallory would have some genius plan. Declaring the Harbour sovereign territory. Merging it with Estonia, or something. But she, too, was only human.

'Where's this healthy paranoia coming from, anyway?' she asked.

'I'm ... I'm worried that something happens before I'm done. Before I figure out what went wrong.'

Her gaze softened a little. 'How are the experiments going?'

'Oh. Good. Running a set of mRNA reaction conditions, to see if that was the problem.'

She frowned. 'You are thinking polymerase errors. Introducing random splicing sites. Dominant negative final product to squash whatever p53 your mom had left?'

I nodded. Mallory drummed the rough table surface with her clawlike fingers. 'That seems a bit too random,' she said. 'Also, splicing is cell-type dependent, so you might never

19

reproduce it *in vitro*. Wait. This was circular mRNA, right? To improve stability?'

'Yeah,' I said. It had been my idea. Mom and I had struggled to get the mRNA to last long enough in her cells. I had found an old patent for making mRNA circles. Gluing the mRNA ends together protected it from the enzymes that chewed it up in the body.

'OK. I have another thought. Come by the lab tomorrow and we can talk about it.'

I looked away, a lump in my throat. She was actually offering to help. But if I stayed, I would put everything she had been building at risk.

Mallory leaned forward. 'Hey. Fuck that self-pity shit. You *will* figure this out. It's obviously going to work. Your mother and I didn't always see eye to eye, but she had guts.' She lifted her beer in a silent toast and took a sip. 'Life might feel like hell now, but hell's just another step in the protocol.'

'Hello, ladies!'

Jerome sat back down and put a pint glass and a steaming plate of food in front of me – mammoth brisket and sweet potato mash. The rich smell made my mouth water and reminded me of how hungry I was. He also passed me a microneedle patch, a Band-Aid-like thing with a cheerful skull pattern.

'Figured you might be behind on your updates,' he said. One of Jerome's odd jobs was to help run the vaccine printer in the lab barge.

I weighed the patch between my fingers. This was how the Harbour managed without Aspises: community-made vaccines against the latest Plagues in circulation, updated once a month. A dedicated subDarkome designed them using public sequencing data. In spite of what I had told Dad, they were not perfect. Dad and half the Harbour had caught a CEREM-V variant last winter. It caused vivid, uncontrollable dreams. The aftereffects might have contributed to Dad's sleep deprivation after Mom died.

I thought about the Aspis chip and its instant immune updates. Maybe things would have been different if we had never come here. Maybe Mom would still be alive and able to enrol in PROSPERITY-A.

But right now, no matter what happened next, I was still here. I unwrapped the patch and pressed it down on my forearm. It tingled a bit, but was much less painful than the intramuscular mRNA jabs from my childhood.

'Hello?' Jerome said. 'Earth to Inara?'

'Sorry,' I said. 'I do need some food.' I dug into the brisket and the gamey flavours exploded in my mouth, perfectly complemented by the creamy mash. Darin was getting better at the texture. The meat came from a stainless steel bioreactor in the Dark Star's pantry.

'Be my guest,' Jerome said and leaned his elbows on the table. 'I didn't get around to telling you, but we are actually celebrating.' He nodded at Mallory, who raised her pint glass again. 'I proposed a beach rave, but Mallory likes things low-key.'

'Celebrating what?' I asked through mouthfuls of food.

'Shit. You *have* been out of the loop.' He lowered his voice. 'We did it. We stole the weights for Kintu. Enigma Labs' foundation model. They are now on Darkome. We're going to have our own jailbroken AI for the whole community.' Jerome's lopsided grin was radiant.

I stared at Jerome. This wasn't good.

'What do you say to that? Cutting edge model, billion dollars in training. And now everyone can use it.'

I put down my fork. 'That's ... cool, I guess. How on earth did you pull it off?'

'Ha, Inara Reyes is not easily impressed, I see!' He leaned forward and drew shapes in the air with his long fingers. 'Get this. Keystroke-capturing biofilm. We cloned voltage-sensitive proteins into *Bacillus subtilis* that trigger a DNA ligase. Like a molecular tape recorder. Then we hung around the Enigma HQ in Berkeley and sprayed it around on surfaces in coffee shops and places where the technical staff have lunch. You know these nerds, they are obsessed with mechanical keyboards. Perfect places for our babies to grow. And the best part? They sporulate. Boom!'

He threw his arms up. 'Spores are invisible. Spores stick on clothes. We – and by we, I mean me – brush up against people coming out of the building, and sequence what sticks. You don't get *every* keystroke, of course, but it's enough negentropy for Mallory here to go to town on brute-forcing passwords. I honestly didn't think it would work, too many moving parts. But I guess we are simply that good.' He winked at Mallory, who rolled her eyes.

My mind raced. This made everything worse. If Dad drew public attention to the Harbour and Darkome and there was an investigation, they would find a direct DNA trail from the Enigma theft to Jerome and Mallory.

'Does Holst know about this?'

Mallory pursed her lips. 'Holst and I have an understanding. He takes care of the Harbour's soul, and I make the trains run on time.'

'Come on, Inara,' Jerome said. 'This is big. In fact – do you want to go out, afterwards? I'm meeting some friends from Oakland later. There is a big party in the old Naval Depot—'

Suddenly, Jerome and Mallory's voices receded into the distance. The Dark Star felt like a fragile bubble of warmth between the darkness of the sea and the hills. I looked around me, lost in thought.

Darin, the burly harbourmaster with a twirled Dalí moustache, was chatting with Holst by the stage. I sipped the beer he had crafted for me, a non-alcoholic stout with traces of gene therapy viruses. The idea had been to tolerise my body to them, but I'd come to enjoy the taste. Darin had a unique brew for everyone, even Dad. In the back, Z, Lorena, and Maya were playing with Lorena's interactive biofilm wall. It responded to touch. You could use your fingertip to draw bright lines that changed colour unpredictably. The trio's game was some kind of mad Pictionary where two players drew together, trying to co-ordinate silently, with the third player guessing. They were all past middle age but laughing like children. The wall behind them blazed with swirling shapes like psychedelic galaxies.

And then I saw Dad, sitting by himself near the edge of the beer garden, watching me.

Cold certainty descended on me. There was no way I could allow all this to disappear, no matter the cost.

'One second,' I told Jerome. 'I need the restroom.'

I walked over to Dad. His face was drawn, but the resolve was still there in his eyes. I put my palms on the scuffed table and leaned towards him.

'You win,' I said coldly. 'I'll do it. But let me have tonight. We can leave tomorrow.'

23

His expression was a mixture of relief and pain. He nodded and got up. 'I'll start packing.' His hands twitched, as if he was about to reach out and touch me. But he simply stuffed them into his pockets and trudged away, without looking back.

I wanted to scream again, but held it in. I went to the Dark Star's all-gender restroom and sat in one of the stalls with hands clamped over my mouth until the need to howl faded. Then I walked back to the Dark Star's warmth for one last time.

Back at our table, Jerome had switched to whisky and was gesticulating wildly at Kieran, who had joined our table. He had been a major figure in the jetpack racing circuit back in the day, but now he was trying to solve human-powered flight – how to actually give humans wings.

'And then we had to figure out how to actually find a reference genome for these spores – Inara!' I flashed him a microsecond smile. 'Sorry to interrupt,' I said and grabbed his hand. 'We need to talk.'

He flashed a thumbs-up to Kieran as I dragged him away. Jerome had never been good at holding his liquor.

We shared a kiss in the Dark Star's small parking lot, by the giant bee. Jerome's new beard tickled, but I could still feel his scar underneath. He pushed a hand under my shirt, traced fumbling circles on my belly.

'We're almost at my place,' he whispered, kissing my neck. 'We don't have to go back.'

I bit my lip. More than anything, I wanted to get lost in the smooth warmth of his skin. It would be so easy, so familiar, so good.

So good that I'd never be able to leave him.

I took a deep breath and cupped his cheek firmly. 'Jerome,' I said. 'I have to tell you something.'

'Come on, Inara,' he said, hugging me close. 'I've *missed* you. And it's such a great night. You know I'm going to be on DzoGene's show?'

'What?'

'It's true. He reached out after we published the Kintu weights on Darkome.'

Now I could see why Jerome was so giddy. DzoGene was a Darkome celebrity, especially with the more extreme Transhumanist set. Jerome was obsessed with his casts and had made me watch them too. Listening to an anthropomorphic Siberian fox avatar interview human-enhancement focused biohackers was our version of a romantic evening.

'That's ... that's great. I'm happy for you.'

'You don't *sound* happy.' Jerome shook himself like a dog and gave me a more sober look. 'OK. What's wrong, Inara?'

I rubbed my face. Saying it aloud would make it real.

'I'm leaving the Harbour.'

'What? Why?'

'It's ... there's an Aspis trial I'm going to join. It might actually help. But obviously I can't stay here.'

He took a step back. 'Wow. I mean, that ... that is a lot to process, Inara. Are you sure it's the right thing? What about your mom's work?'

'I'm ... I'm sure. And, I need more time to finish it. I can't do that if I get sick.'

He looked down and ran a hand through his thick hair. 'Shit.' Then he brightened. 'But you're not going far, right? It doesn't have to change anything.'

A wild hope leaped in my chest. Maybe we could make it

work. It would be hard – even having sex would be risky, if there were Plagues my new Aspis blocked and Darkome vaccines didn't. But if I stayed in the Bay Area, he'd be mere hours away.

But Jerome worked with Mallory - wanted to be the new Mallory, or DzoGene. I could never tell him why I really had to leave, about Dad's blackmail. My secret would always be between us, a layer no less isolating than the respirators Darkome people had to wear to visit the default world.

I looked into his luminous green eyes and thought about the day I had met him. Darin had forgotten to give him the keys to the old ice cream truck and was out of town, so he had to break in to open up. I came across him shimmying the back doors open. He looked like a lean, scarred lion, with wild hair and a tank top. I thought he was a burglar, grabbed a nearby footstool and nearly brained him with it, but he talked me down and made me a pear ice cream cone. We waited for people to show up, lying in the folding sun chairs next to the truck, in no hurry to go anywhere.

No, it was kinder to keep the memories untainted, make a clean break, right now. I swallowed.

"That's ... that's not what I want right now, Jerome. I need to be alone for a while. I'm sorry."

He said nothing. A part of me wanted him to be unreasonable, to argue, to fight for me. But maybe I had fooled myself into thinking I was worth fighting for.

"Don't worry, it works out well for you," I said, voice colder than I intended. "You'll be the next Darkome celebrity. Best keep your options open."

'Inara,' he said. 'That's not it. I ...'

'It's OK,' I said. 'It's for the best.'

I kissed his scarred cheek. 'Goodbye, Jerome.'

I walked back to the beer garden alone. My chest ached with yet another bone-deep wound, but I kept my eyes dry. I had to, until Dad and I were gone.

Darin had lit some outdoor heaters against the evening chill. I sat back down and finished my food. Now that the Conspiracy of Mustaches' show was over, a bigger group gathered around Mallory's table. Lorena had noticed my bare feet and brought me woolly socks and flipflops. Z tried to get a Dungeons and Dragons game started. Darin took out his mandolin and thrummed light melodies. Holst sat next to Mallory, still wearing his moustache.

I tried to capture it in the amber of memory. The way the socks tickled my ankles. The weight of the d20 in my hand. The laughter in my chest washing over heartbreak like waves over sharp rocks.

People gradually left, one by one, until only Holst and I remained. He sat next to me, hands in his lap. The bench was too low for him and his knees jutted out, locust-like. His ancient horse-face was melancholy, but that was how he always looked. I felt safe and calm, held by the warm space around him.

I wanted to say a hundred things. Thank him for letting my family in. For being a good friend, for creating the Harbour in the first place. Say how sorry I was for endangering it. Ask him what the hell he thought the fungi were going to say, once he finally figured out how to talk to them.

He smiled gently. I realised that somehow, he already knew I was leaving. Maybe Dad had talked to him, or Jerome, or the mycelium. It didn't matter.

He reached out a long arm and gently drew me into an

27

embrace. I leaned my head on his shoulder. He smelled of hiking sweat and redwood trees.

'I am going to come back, I swear. I will find a way.'

'Does the wave ever leave the ocean?' he asked.

'Save me the hippie bullshit, Holst,' I said, tearing up. 'Tell me straight. Is there no way I can stay? Can't you bend the rules, just this once? What harm can one Aspis do?'

Holst looked sombre. 'I'm sorry, Inara. The Harbour is like a foetus. Its immune system is still developing. We must take care over what we expose it to, what becomes self and non-self. For now, we need rules to define us. Mallory would never let me break them.'

He patted my back gently. 'But things change. We accept the alien and grow. Even the gene that allowed your mother to carry you came from an ancient infection. Maybe you are the virus that lets us be born. Give it time, Inara. Give it time.'

3

The Protocol

It was well past midnight when I made it back to the *Maré Viva*. Dad was packing furiously, throwing things into cardboard boxes strewn across the floor. The entire lab corner was untouched, though. He stood up with a grunt when I entered, a hand on the small of his back.

For a moment, we stared at each other. Then he looked away.

'It's too much to finish tonight,' he said. 'When we are settled, I'll come back and put it all in storage, and put the houseboat on sale.'

'Settled where?'

'Mojave. I've got a job in the Reclamation Project. Doesn't pay that well, but the accommodation is free. And the foundation has scholarship programmes for college. You ... you might like it there, Inara.'

'Yeah,' I said quietly. 'I might.'

We packed in silence, moving past each other in the cramped houseboat like ghosts. I had filled a small backpack with essentials and a dry ice cooler with reagents. Then I checked Mom's cells.

They were all dying, every single well. I had learned nothing.

I packed them in the cooler anyway.

We left early in the morning, in Dad's old Dodge Charger, while the Harbour still slept. We drove up the brambly hillside road, past the empty warehouses, the train track that led nowhere. Gradually, the desolation was replaced by suburbs and parkland.

When we were almost in San Rafael, I put on my Aspis. I braced myself for a sting, but it stuck to my skin painlessly. The stretchy nylon strap had that new-electronics smell. I installed the Aspis app and opened it in my Eyes. Everything was already set up for me to enrol in PROSPERITY-A.

I eyeclicked through the forms. The data consent gave me pause. In order to design on-the-fly mRNA vaccines targeting early cancer markers in my body, the chip needed access to single cell resolution data. Aspis had the rights to any IP generated from it. It made me sick. I was going to be a ghoul, in the thrall of a master vampire who fed on my blood.

Dad had already signed. I gritted my teeth and added my signature.

Finally, the app showed me a short greeting video from Amanda Shah, Aspis's CEO. She was in her mid-forties, a solid, dark-haired woman with a permanent frown. There were redwood trees behind her. She looked awkward in front of the camera and did not quite manage a smile. She wore a black T-shirt and a puffy North Face jacket. Wikipedia claimed that was her only outfit.

'Thank you for joining PROSPERITY-A,' she said. Her brown-eyed gaze was unsettlingly intense, piercing even through the screen. 'It takes courage to try something new.

30

And we need something new. Cancer continues to profoundly affect patients and families all around the world.'

No shit, I thought. I only knew her Wikipedia summary – Indian immigrant parents, grew up in Berkeley, child prodigy, Thiel Fellow. It could have been an AI-generated stereotype of a deep tech founder. *Good. Let's keep it that way. She is the enemy. No need to make her human.*

'At Aspis, we have been unwavering in our commitment to bring the same technologies we built to prevent pandemics to preventing cancer. This trial is our flagship effort to do so. By participating, you are helping patients like you take a big step towards a world where freedom from cancer is a fundamental human right—'

She droned on. I clenched my fists. I tried to pour all my rage at her. She was a better enemy than Dad: someone I could allow myself to fully hate.

But I had no anger left. The Aspis had drained it from me with the tiny drops of blood it took to steal what made me human.

Only what needed to be done remained.

I closed the Aspis app and took off my Eyes.

'Dad?' I said. 'I'd like to go visit Mom.'

He nodded and steered off the highway, to Rolling Hills Memorial Park. We had picked the closest cemetery that laid Catholics to rest, but it had turned out to be a vast expanse with glorious grounds and views of the Bay. The proverbial hills were dotted with structures from flat markers to outright monuments and family mausoleums. There were solitary trees, flower beds and shrubs, all well tended.

We parked. I took my backpack and the cooler. Dad frowned, but said nothing. We walked up the hill to the

31

small headstone that said MANUELA REYES – BELOVED WIFE AND MOTHER. I breathed in the freshly mown grass smell. We hadn't had Aspises at the funeral, so we and the rest of the Harbour crowd had worn respirators. The murmur of the priest's prayers had mixed with my own laboured breathing, and I had only smelled plastic.

The headstone had fresh flowers and candles. I looked at Dad. He shrugged. 'She liked peonies,' he said. 'I bring them every now and then.'

I took the cell culture plate out from the cooler. I crouched down and dug a shallow indentation in the dirt with my hands. I placed the plate there and covered it carefully. The dirt felt alive beneath my fingers. Something of her had to be in it, I thought. She couldn't be all gone.

I gritted my teeth against tears.

'I'm sorry I couldn't figure it out, Mom,' I said. 'But I will. I promise.' *And I'm sorry for what I'm about to do.*

'I'll give you a minute,' Dad said. 'I'll go wait in the car.'

I stood up and wiped my hands on my jeans.

'Dad. I'm not coming.'

He blinked. 'What do you mean?'

'I'm not coming to Mojave with you. I don't know where I'm going, yet. But it's not there, and it's not with you.'

'Inara, I'm so sorry, I—'

'I'm going to be OK, Dad. And so will you. Don't worry, I'll keep the Aspis and stay in the trial, as long as I need to. I still have a little money from Mom's life insurance.' I took a deep breath. 'But for now, I need to be free. I hope you understand that.' My chest hurt with anger. 'And if you don't, well ...' I glanced at Mom's headstone. 'You can grow potatoes in China.'

His shoulders slumped. He opened his mouth to say something, then closed it. 'Be safe, OK?' he said. 'I love you, Inara.' His voice broke.

I nodded. He backed away, as if he couldn't look away from me, but finally turned around and ambled down the hill, faster as he went, almost breaking into a run.

I waited until he was out of earshot before I let the tears come.

I sat with Mom for a while, listening to the birds. Then I gathered my things and started walking. It was a long way to somewhere with enough signal to call a self-drive. The Aspis felt heavy on my arm, my backpack dug into my shoulders, and the bright sunlight made my head hurt like hell.

I kept going.

Hell was just another step in the protocol.

Part Two

The Haunted House, 2041

4

Unleashed

Two years later, on the day I found the Heffalump in my breast, I got myself fired.

It was 9 a.m. on the Wildcat Peak Trail in Tilden Regional Park. Clementine, my BarkButler client, raced ahead on the woody path on a long leash. Her smart collar captured her joy and transmitted it to the Senselet in my wrist as a pleasant tingle. That was one of the reasons I had originally signed up. Dog happiness drowned out the constant murmur of my oncosense – most of the time, anyway.

But today, the wind brought the woodbrick barbecue smell of Napa wildfires, full of carcinogens. My skin prickled with the oncosense's insects-on-skin feeling. I could tell the risk scores even without looking at the widget in my Eyes. 20 per cent chance of glioblastoma in the next five years. My old friend osteosarcoma, hovering close to 10 per cent. PROSPERITY-A was running a secondary trial to see if constant peripheral awareness of cancer risk led to positive behavioural change. I had joined it to remind myself that my fight wasn't over.

Clementine and I emerged from the woods to a bare

37

hillside. I have to be pretty careful in the sun and wore a long-sleeved black top with a Giants cap. The dry June heat hit me hard. I was sweating within minutes, but the scenery was worth the sting of SPF100 suncream in my eyes. I stopped to give Clementine water from a foldable cup. She lapped at it eagerly while I took in the view. Sunburnt trees covered gentle hills. The Bay Bridge arced over dark waters. San Francisco's towers rose from a white expanse of morning fog that covered the city. I had five more walks lined up, not to mention an hour-long commute. But there were some perks to being a parasite on the Bay Area's wealthy overclass.

Most importantly, it paid enough to keep me close to the Harbour. That was also the reason I did this particular hike with Clementine at least once a week. There was a clear view of Point San Pablo from the summit. I could zoom in with my Eyes and see the only place where I had ever really belonged.

Suddenly, Clementine tugged at the leash hard. A discarded energy bar wrapper lay on the trail. She snapped it up in her mouth.

'Clementine, no.' I yanked the leash. 'Leave it!'

She dropped the wrapper, lowered her head and wagged her tail apologetically. The neosense pulsated with her shame. I swore quietly. That was probably half a star off my BarkButler rating for this walk.

To make amends, I gave her a cultured bison treat from my belt pouch. She flashed me a dog grin and pounded up the steep trail.

It was hard to believe she was seventeen years old – eighty in human years. The thick white Canigen collar around her neck had completely transformed her in the last couple of months, from a doddering old lady into a glossy-coated whirlwind.

Aspis had spun out Canigen a year ago, after the bad guys had switched their attention from humans to pets. I couldn't exactly fault Clementine's owner Kathryn for getting one. I would have paid through the nose to prevent *my* dog from catching a designer ransomware virus. And that was before Canigen started rolling out the anti-ageing payloads. It was obvious Aspis was building up to it with their flagship human product too, as soon as the FDA would let them. And as a clinical trial participant, I was helping them.

The old anger buzzed in my head, suddenly. Those bastards got to decide what went into my body. Yes, they kept me cancer-free, but also had me tethered to their damn chip. I scratched the thin white disc of the Aspis beneath my sleeve like an itching scar. I was every bit as much on a leash as Clementine was. I hated myself for not daring to rip it off. But even after two years of work, I was no closer to figuring out what had gone wrong with Mom than the day she died.

And so here I was: scraping together a living, hanging out in subDarkomes and telling myself that one day, I would figure it out and return to the Harbour in triumph, with fully working p53 in my cells, Aspis-free. In the meantime, Aspis kept making the world less and less like the one I wanted to live in.

The heat transformed my anger into wild elation like an alchemist's oven. Something inside me wanted to run.

'Clementine,' I called. She came to me, head down, still looking a little bashful. I bent down and unclipped the leash from her collar. I could give her a taste of freedom, Kathryn's BarkButler preferences be damned.

'Let's go.'

I sprinted forward. Clementine's joy exploded in the Senselet. I used it to go faster, past a copse of trees, up a steep slope with thick roots like stairs. We flashed past a shirtless jogger, but I barely noticed him through the black dots swimming in my eyes.

Finally, I had to stop. I bent over, leaned on my knees and fought nausea. We were almost at the summit. The green hills of Tilden Park lay past the ridge ahead. Clementine ran rings around me, celebrating life with every wag of her tail. I laughed between breaths. It felt like we had outrun death itself.

Then a large black Rottweiler male trundled up the trail towards us.

Clementine perked up. She struck a playful pose – front paws extended, butt up – and yipped at him. He didn't like it. The hair on his thick neck bristled.

'Clementine, come!' I shouted. Before the Canigen, her recall had been perfect. But now she ignored me.

The other dog's head snapped, and Clementine let out a yowl. Almost simultaneously, the Senselet stung my wrist. Still wheezing, I stumbled towards them.

'Clementine!' The Rottweiler lunged at her, and not in a playful way. Clementine fell on her back and bared her throat. They rolled in the dust. The black dog's jaws latched around Clementine's neck. He seized her and flung her from side to side like a rag doll. The Senselet buzzed madly. The BarkButler widget in my Eyes exploded with alerts.

A desperate strength surged through my legs. I covered the remaining distance in seconds.

'Get off!'

I grabbed the dogs' collars and tried to pull them apart. The whites of Clementine's eyes showed and her mouth foamed. The Rottweiler let go and snapped at my hand. His paws scrabbled on the gravel. He tried to lunge at Clementine again and almost pulled me off my feet, but I held firm. She retreated behind me, tail between her legs.

Then the jogger was there, looking at us from a hundred feet away. 'Hey!' I shouted at him while gulping air. 'Control ... your ... fucking ... animal!' The BarkButler app was recording video now and a red dot blinked at the edge of my vision.

The man gestured, and the Rottweiler stiffened. He had a shock collar, I realised. The black dog yanked away from me and shot down the trail. Without a word, the owner turned round and followed.

'Asshole!' I shouted. The BarkButler app recorded that, too, but I didn't care.

Once I got my breath back, I inspected Clementine. She was shaking, but did not seem seriously hurt. The worst was a small, bloodless toothmark in her left ear. I stroked her to calm her down. She licked my cheek. 'OK. You're OK, girl,' I whispered. We both were. Clementine's owner Kathryn liked me. I could take the one-star rating. It was going to be fine.

And then Clementine started wheezing.

The corners of her mouth twisted into a fearful dog smile. She took laborious, rasping breaths and rubbed her nose with a paw.

Fuck.

The BarkButler AI popped up a message window.

> LIKELY TRACHEAL DAMAGE, it said. > STAY CALM. ALERTING VETERINARY CLINIC AT 400 UNIVERSITY AVENUE NOW.

Stay calm. OK. Boxed breathing. *Breath in, one, two, three, four. Hold, one, two, three, four. Breath out, one, two, three, four.*

My head cleared, and the BarkButler dog first-aid training came back to me. Clementine's windpipe was bruised and swelling. I needed to create more space in the airway.

I wrapped my arms around her in a soothing embrace. She squirmed, but allowed me to press her down to lie on her side. Her ribs rose and fell rapidly, and her breath sounded even thinner. I cradled her head to extend her neck. That seemed to help a bit. I pushed a finger past her back teeth, probing for obstructions in her throat. She twitched and almost bit my finger off. I yanked it out, soothed and stroked, tried again. This time, she coughed out a gobbet of drool and blood. Then she lay still, panting. Her breathing was still laboured, but no longer wheezing.

The block of ice in my gut thawed a little. I kept monitoring Clementine, ready to give her rescue breaths if needed. At the same time, I scanned through the BarkButler list of messages in my Eyes. Help was on the way. If Clementine didn't get worse in the next few minutes, it should be safe to move her. I could lead or carry her to the trailhead to meet the vet and their vehicle.

As Clementine's breath steadied, my own grew shallow. What the hell had I been thinking? Letting a dog off the leash was a company policy violation. I was toast. BarkButlers didn't let the few precious dogs who had survived the Decade of Plagues get into fights. And it wasn't just the job. Clementine was a living being under my care, and I had fucked up.

Clementine's tongue lolled out. Her tail beat at the ground weakly. My chest felt cold and hollow.

'I'm sorry,' I said. 'Looks like this was our last walk.'

I ruffled her ears and held her close. Her affection radiated from the Senselet, and suddenly, I realised what had changed.

There were no crawling insects on my scalp. No constant red alert, no pop-up risk scores, no anxious whispers.

My oncosense was completely quiet.

5

The Haunted House

Very slowly, I half-led, half-carried Clementine back down to the trailhead. Staying focused on her kept me from panicking. Every ping from the BarkButler app made my heart jump.

A sturdy African American vet in a BarkButler T-shirt was waiting for us next to a Rivian pick-up truck. The woman briskly inspected Clementine and concluded she was not in any immediate danger. Clementine got an mRNA shot of a growth factor to accelerate healing, and then the vet loaded her into the back of the car. She scraped the window with a paw and whined.

'Guess I should see the other guy, huh?' the vet said and winked. She saw my expression and grew serious. 'Hey. You all good here?'

'Yeah,' I said. My stomach was a queasy pit. 'All good.'

She nodded, got into the car and sped away, sending gravel flying. I stared at Clementine's golden form in the back window until they disappeared behind a bend.

A dinky BarkButler self-drive picked me up a few minutes after that. I sat in the back seat that smelled of stale fast food and dictated a statement into my Eyes. My own voice sounded distant as I described my efforts to separate the dogs and the first-aid steps.

Then there was nothing left to do except to watch the wheels spin. The app informed me that Clementine's owner, Kathryn, had been notified. Clementine would be kept overnight at the clinic for observation, and BarkButler's insurance would cover the bill. Kathryn would be compensated for the distress caused. Whether I was liable for that or not depended on the outcome of an AI mediation process between the insurer and BarkButler, based on the recording and my statement.

Oh, and my contract as a BarkButler was terminated due to a gross policy violation, effective immediately.

I folded the screen and stared out of the window. For a moment, I considered apologising to Kathryn in person. I imagined facing her in her glass and concrete home on its elevated perch in Berkeley Hills, Kathryn hugging herself with yoga-toned arms, eyes flint-hard in her tanned face. What would I even say? *I'm sorry, my oncosense malfunctioned, so I went a bit nuts and let your dog loose.* I shook my head. It was pointless. She had enough to worry about without a sweaty mutant girl spouting nonsense at her.

I dropped off my gear at BarkButler's service centre on Shattuck Avenue in downtown Berkeley. It didn't take long. The uniform, the treat bag, the whistle, the leash reels and the rest went into a storage locker, no human interaction required. Then I was free, BarkButler no more.

I was unmoored from my routine and had no idea what to do with myself. I wandered into the nearby Civic Center Park, but the temperature was creeping into the 90s

45

Fahrenheit, and the manicured lawns were packed with students. Exhausted, I looked up the nearest MysteryMobile stop to catch a ride home. Thankfully, one came by in a few minutes. They were fractionally owned buses that us glitzers (BarkButlers, nannies, chefs and others of our kind) used to get around outside work. This one was a battered Tesla TransitMax minibus, and only had half a dozen people on board.

I grabbed a plush seat close to the central touchscreen, next to a voluptuous, middle-aged woman who had her Eyes in full mirrorshade VR mode, probably on Illusia. I took out my own smartglasses and was putting them on when I realised she wore a Zephyra Lux T-shirt.

It showed a brief clip from one of her last gigs. Zephyra was wearing her iconic outfit, a plain white tank top and shorts, but her face, her shaven scalp, her belly, her arms and legs all pulsed with patters of kaleidoscopic luminescence. It wasn't a special effect. Her skin was full of fluorescent sound-responsive proteins that reacted to the music, to her own voice, to the roar of the audience. She was made of living light.

I looked at the glitzer lady's slack face, lost in a generative AI daydream, and something snapped in me.

'Hey.' I grabbed the woman's arm and shook her. She jerked. Her Eyes flashed to transparency. She blinked for a second, and then her face twisted in anger.

'What the hell?'

'Zephyra would have hated you wearing that while on Illusia,' I said. 'Have some fucking respect.'

'Jesus H Christ,' she said. 'Knew her *personally*, did you?'

I blinked. What was *wrong* with me? Of course I hadn't.

I'd seen her Darkome AMA. She had been awesome, edgy and funny and irreverent. But I had never been able to even afford a ticket to her live gigs.

'No, but—'

'Then I don't give a damn. I'm a Workmate, little miss. This shirt is a conversation starter to get the nerds talking to me. And you cost me a minute of Illusia time, so you and Miss Lux can fuck right off. If you love her so much, go inject yourself with some shit and die like she did.'

The sudden guilt and memory of Mom stung like a slap. My cheeks burned. Zephyra had died three months ago, after dosing herself with mRNA that was supposed to enhance empathy. Darkome rumours claimed her Aspis had misidentified it as a virus and triggered an autoimmune reaction – or even that Aspis had targeted her deliberately. For obvious reasons, I had spent a few weeks on subDarkomes, obsessing over her fate.

The woman folded her arms, leaned back and her Eyes became opaque silvery orbs again. 'Some nerve,' she muttered.

I slunk back in my chair and pushed my cap down to avoid the looks from the other glitzers in the car. *Get a hold of yourself, Inara,* I thought. *She's right. You have better things to worry about than a stranger's T-shirt.*

Like making a living.

The TransitMax sped through Oakland and then, predictably, slowed to a crawl on the Bay Bridge. I watched the dark Bay waters and the miniature Spanish galleon model near Angel Island while we made our way through the jam.

Maybe Dad had been right all along. Maybe making my own cure was hopeless. Even people like Zephyra with every possible resource managed to fuck their bodies up. Dad might have kept his promise and stayed quiet about Mom, but Zephyra's death had been high profile enough that the authorities finally took a closer look at Darkome. Congressman Jake Kim — who policy subDarkomes claimed was in Amanda Shah's pocket — had even introduced a draft bill called the Zephyra Lux Act that was supposed to strengthen regulations around biohacking. Shah herself was scheduled to appear at a committee hearing in a week.

Most pundits thought it was posturing, a way for politicians to highlight their views on biosecurity before the midterms, and would never get bipartisan support. Still, it was entirely possible the Harbour I wanted to go back to would not even exist in a year or two.

Maybe I should call it a day, go to the Midwest or Mojave, live on universal basic and volunteer for the big climate projects.

Maybe it was time to grow up.

The fury that had made me unleash Clementine and grab the Workmate woman's arm was back. Fuck despair, said a voice that was like Mallory's. Fuck self-pity. Fuck the Feds. All this is preparing you, making you stronger.

'Just another step in the protocol,' I muttered.

Remembering that cleared my head. Something was off. Why did I keep losing control? And what was up with my oncosense? The obvious theory was that the damn Rottweiler had broken my Senselet. But the pink ouroboros around my wrist had no visible physical damage. The other neosenses I had installed seemed to be working fine, too.

I put on my Eyes and rebooted the Senselet, following the how-tos overlaid on the little device. Then I re-installed the oncosense app and re-paired it with my Aspis. Still nothing. Even twisting the bracelet's little metal crown to turn the neosense intensity to maximum had no effect.

I frowned. There was a mystery here, and I owed it to both Clementine and myself to solve it. But debugging the Aspis itself had to wait until I was home.

I got off at the stop at the bottom of Dolores Heights. I didn't usually do the long fifty-degree climb in the brutal midday heat, and by the time I reached the top, my legs were done and I was drenched in sweat.

The Haunted House stood blue and tall on Alvarado Street, among ageing tech mansions. Its angular wooden facade had a touch of the Gothic. The name dated back to the Plagues. Back then, the wealthy had fled the city again and ghost workers had moved in – cheap digital labour for data curation and AI alignment training. But now it was a glitzer house. The ghosts were gone, and only murals of white apparitions and spiderwebs remained.

I opened the door with a House token and took my shoes off in the hallway. Thanh, who owned the largest share of the house, was a stickler about that. It felt strange to be back so early. The house was empty and quiet, not surprising since all of us except Thanh and Svetlana mostly worked regular daylight hours. A sharp smell of tomato sauce wafted from the kitchen. Thanh was making her shakshuka, or what she called shakshuka – canned tomatoes mixed with egg in a non-stick pan. As far as I could tell, that was the only thing she ate.

I realised I was ravenous and wandered in to raid the fridge. The kitchen was too small for all ten of us: a stove without a hood, pale beech counters and cheap Ikea furniture. Thanh was sitting at the long dining table, eyes glazed over, earbuds firmly in her ears, flicking through a feed on her folded Eyes with one delicate finger.

She was in day off mode, toned body hidden in a soft grey tracksuit, her lustrous midnight hair in a tight bun, and wearing a silk face mask. She worked as an escort and had frequent face remodels to look like her clients' Illusia characters. Her large green eyes alone were strikingly, inhumanly attractive, but it was really hard to take your eyes off an unmasked Thanh – and so she usually kept covered up at home.

The tomato sauce bubbled on the stove, close to burning. I went over and turned it down to keep the fire alarm from going off. Thanh gave me a cursory wave without looking up. I nodded and opened the large steel fridge. It was overstuffed with Arjun's enormous plastic tubs of spinach, Thanh's egg cartons and all the rest. I grabbed one of my Joylent bottles – and noticed a plastic container with a Post-it note on it that said INARA. It was filled with what looked like fish stew.

I took it out and waved at Thanh. She frowned and took out her earbuds, crossing her manicured fingers beneath her chin.

'What's this?' I asked, lifting the container, even though I knew the answer.

'Your dad dropped it off,' she said. Thanh and I weren't close, but she knew things weren't cordial between me and Dad. 'Looks like he is back in town.' She pointed to the container I was holding. 'What is that thing, anyway? Looks like vomit.'

'Moqueca,' I said quietly. 'Brazilian fish stew. It was my mom's favourite.'

Iron bands of rage tightened around my temples. Why did he keep doing this? He had eventually given up on the video messages, but it sounded like his new Mojave Bloom project job involved coming to SF frequently for some outreach thing, so now he simply turned up. Last time I had stayed in my room until he went away. Thanh had provided poker-faced cover.

'Oh,' Thanh said.

'Yeah.'

I couldn't bring myself to throw the container away and put it back into the fridge. Eventually, bacteria would turn it into something one of my housemates would be forced to dispose of.

Thanh got up and turned off the shakshuka. She stirred it with a spoon into a sort of red eggy porridge and held it up.

'Do you want some?' she asked.

I shook my head. I lifted my Joylent bottle, opened it and downed half of the vanilla-flavoured meal replacement in one go.

Thanh looked at me, cocked her head to one side and frowned. 'You're back early today.'

All of us technically owned a chunk of the Haunted House. I had used the rest of Mom's life insurance as a cash advance for a fractional share that gave me a private room and access to shared spaces. But with the controlling stake, Thanh was, for all practical purposes, our landlady.

I swallowed a mouthful of Joylent, thinking fast.

'Got a bunch of cancellations today,' I said. 'Some new dog virus going around. Not everybody has Canigens yet.'

'Uh huh.' She sat down at the table, faced away from me, took off her mask and started eating the red mess straight from the pot.

'I hope it picks back up for you. Got a couple of new applicants. Extreme sports location scout, very cool lady. And' – Thanh looked up – 'I think some kind of meditation teacher for toddlers? Not sure. Great earning potential, though.'

'They sound great,' I said flatly. We both knew perfectly well that the house was full, and she would have to buy someone out to take in a new partner/tenant.

Unless someone defaulted on their monthly payments, of course.

'Oh – I finally found good contractors for the solar shade installation,' Thanh said. 'They're coming next week. We'll go over the costs in the house meeting.'

I said nothing. The green roofing and solar shade project had been sucking funds from everyone, including me, for almost a year now. Thanh smelled something was up, and probed for an opening. I knew it was nothing personal, she was a shark swimming towards the scent of blood, but it had already been a long day.

'It *is* hot and smelly here,' I said and opened the door to our tiny back garden with a forceful yank.

Thanh put her mask on and turned to look at me, glorious eyes completely deadpan. 'It sure is,' she said. 'The bathroom is free, you know. Go have a long bath.'

I wiped my mouth with my T-shirt sleeve.

'You know what,' I said. 'I think I will.'

'Thank yoooouuuu.'

I tossed the empty Joylent bottle into recycling and

headed for the door. Thanh gave me a little wave. 'Enjoy,' she said. 'And stay cool.'

I climbed the two storeys to my small room. Inside, I immediately breathed more easily. A post-Jerome fling had described it as the Batman villain Two-Face in bedroom form. The bed was in the far corner. Most of my clothes were piled on a rickety wooden chair or on the floor. I used a beanbag for actual sitting.

In contrast, the lab bench by the window was obsessively tidy, crammed with second-hand equipment. I had a PCR machine, a centrifuge, storage boxes for plastics, a microfluidic cell sorter – and, of course, my trusty Eppendorf in a place of honour. On the windowsill behind it sat Jerome's wind-up seahorse, made from twisted copper wire and old gears.

I watered the potted plants on the tiny balcony, the main reason I had picked the room. I was tempted to take a break, enjoy the cloudless sky and watch the world go by. But Thanh had a point. With ten housemates, extended access to one of our two bathrooms was an almost unimaginable luxury.

I undressed, grabbed a fraying bathrobe and a towel from a wall hook, and went to take a bath.

The bigger bathroom on the second floor was my favourite and I barricaded myself in it whenever I got a chance. I kept a small stack of paperbacks there, which drove Svetlana (whose room was across the hallway) nuts. It had the original Victorian wainscoting, chequered floor tiles and a giant ancient clawfoot bathtub. I set the bath running and took off the bathrobe. Force of habit kicked in, and I started running through the self-examination routine I had done at least every month since I was twelve.

I stood in front of the mirror, arms at my sides. A pale girl stared back, hair falling over the café au lait macule on her forehead, wide hips, muscular legs, medium boobs. I zoomed in on my chest. No visible lumps or bumps on the skin or around the nipple. I raised my arms above my head and looked for the same changes. Nothing. I placed my hands firmly on my hips and flexed my chest muscles. Nothing unusual. Fine.

I stole some of Svetlana's bath salts and poured them into the full bathtub. I luxuriated in the foamy, lavender-scented water. I tried to lie still, but my hands moved on their own and completed the check-up.

I was about to relax when my left hand touched something in the edge of my breast, beneath my arm. A patch of tissue slightly firmer than the rest.

I shivered in spite of the gentle heat of the bath. I squeezed the fold of flesh, lost the less pliable part for a second, sighed in relief.

Then I found it again.

I retraced every step of the routine, a weight on my chest. In the end, there was no denying it.

There was a small lump in my left breast.

6

The Heffalump

'Fuck,' I whispered. My hands shook.

For two years, I had been telling myself that any hope for a miracle was false, but the disappointment in my gut was still so sharp that I wanted to throw up.

I had left the Harbour for nothing.

I forced myself to do boxed breathing. In, one, two, three, four. Hold, one, two, three, four. Out, one, two, three, four. I lost track of time doing it, but when I could think clearly again, the water was cool.

I rubbed the Aspis on my upper arm. There it sat, embedded in my skin like a high-tech tick. Its sole LED blinked green. It made no sense. If I had so much cancerous tissue that I could detect it by touch, how the hell wasn't the Aspis picking up the circulating tumour DNA it had to be shedding by the molecular fuckton?

The obvious answer was that my unit was defective, it had failed to detect and respond to the tumour, and had finally broken down today when my oncosense failed. But that didn't make sense either, even ignoring Aspis's incredibly rigorous FDA-approved manufacturing and quality assurance process. PROSPERITY-A participants got replacement units every month. I'd had this one for less than two weeks, and it would have taken the lump much longer, months at least, to get to this stage.

I pressed the tiny nub under my skin again. 'What are you doing in there, little Heffalump?' I asked aloud, suddenly struck by an image of the elusive elephant-like creature that haunted Winnie the Pooh and Piglet. 'How are you staying hidden?'

Back in my room, cosy in my bathrobe, I sat down at my lab bench. I took the Eppendorf and tossed it back and forth between my post-bath wrinkled, lavender-scented hands. Panic squirmed under my scalp. Call Dr Nguyen right now, it whispered. Get this sorted out now.

And what then? Another surgery scar. Another round of BiTEs – immunotherapies that grabbed cancer cells and shoved them in my immune cells' faces, toxic as hell, months of misery. And then, back on PROSPERITY-A with an updated Aspis, back where I started.

'Like hell,' I said. A cold, angry wind blew through me, and took doubt with it. Mom had been right, and I had wasted enough time. I was going solve this myself, once and for all.

I replaced the pipette in its rack and put my Eyes on. First, eliminating the impossible. I told the PROSPERITY-A bot that my unit was behaving strangely. For all their corporate evilness, they were pretty good about this kind of thing, and promised a replacement within hours.

In the meantime, I leaned back and eyeclicked the Aspis app. The dashboard appeared in my field of vision. Sequencing reagents at 70 per cent, synthesis reagents at

55 per cent, days before a refill was needed. And the chip at least claimed to be talking to Aspis's quantum-encrypted starlink cluster, which it used to upload my data and download the mRNA sequences that went into my body.

Next, I called up the raw Aspis data feed, a streaming wall of letters, all the DNA it found in my bloodstream. That was no good to me by itself so I threw it at Donnie – the Darkome community's own fine-tuned foundation model, built on the one Jerome and Mallory had stolen from Enigma Labs, two years ago. It ingested the million typewriting monkeys' worth of As, Ts, Cs and Gs and turned them into a neat set of fluctuating bubbles, clusters of genes with live annotations.

As far as I could tell, the chip had been working perfectly for the past two weeks. The usual range of pre-cancerous mutations and epigenetic changes showed up, were uploaded into the Aspis cloud and vaccinated against, along with a circulating Plague or two. But any changes associated with breast cancer were conspicuously absent, and none of these data were making it to the Senselet.

I zoomed in to data from today. *There.* Right before 9 a.m., a weird cluster of sequences popped up that had Donnie completely stymied.

Exactly when I had my crazy impulse to let Clementine off the leash.

I stared at the sequences. They were incredibly repetitive, not at all like normal human genes. The only things Donnie could find that were even remotely similar were aptamers, DNA or RNA molecules that folded into weird shapes, involved in the origins of life, pre-dating cells or proteins.

OK. Maybe it was a sequencing error that had triggered some kind of cascading failure. And maybe the Heffalump was a harmless cyst that had nothing to do with cancer. My gut disagreed, but so far, that was the most parsimonious explanation. If it held up, the replacement Aspis would sort everything out, and there was nothing to do but wait.

Suddenly, I felt wrung out. I took off my Eyes, crawled into bed and wrapped myself in the mismatched sheets. Errant thoughts brawled in my head like Clementine and the Rottweiler. I prepared myself for a couple of hours of tossing and turning. But as I was about to reach for the Eyes and the oblivion of Illusia, a heavy blanket of exhaustion settled on me, muffled all mental chatter, and I fell into a deep, dreamless sleep.

A notification ping from the Eyes woke me. It was past 6 p.m., and the sky outside was darkening into indigo. My replacement Aspis had arrived and waited outside the front door. Without bothering to dress, I sprinted downstairs.

Halfway down, I ran into Svetlana. She was kitted out for work, clearly headed to a wine gig of some kind, in a dark pantsuit, a slick raincoat, and leather boots to die for. She gave me a cool blue-eyed look from beneath her groomed eyebrows. 'Hey, Reyes,' she said. 'Did you use the bathroom earlier?'

I shrugged.

'Lots of water on the floor,' she said. 'Like a duck had been taking a bath.'

'Maybe it did,' I said. 'Lots of odd ducks around here.'

'And ugly ducklings,' she said. 'Not all of them swans.'

'Ouch.' I feigned a hurt expression and rubbed my macule. 'As God made me.'

This was a little out of character for Svetlana. We kept our distance: our approaches to tidiness were, shall we say, antipodal, to the extent where close contact could lead to mutual annihilation. Still, she was usually aloof rather than rude.

She ran a hand through her hair, a chic asymmetrical bob that had a geometric pattern on the shaved side. 'Shit. Didn't mean it. Stressful work thing. Sorry.'

I opened my mouth to tell her to piss off. But losing the oncosense and finding Heffalump had left me oddly tender. I sighed. 'It's fine,' I said. 'I know how it is. I'll do a clean there tomorrow. Promise.'

Svetlana blinked. 'That would be great.' She stared at me for a moment. 'Nice ... bathrobe,' she finally said, making a brave attempt at a compliment.

I grinned. 'Seriously, it's fine. Good luck at your thing.'

'Thanks. Ciao.' She glanced at the folded Eyes in her hand and stomped down the stairs like a well-groomed avalanche. I followed, grabbed the AspisCare package from the front door mat and returned to my room.

Taking off the old Aspis felt like pulling off a sticky plaster. It left behind a pattern of tiny red dots on my skin. I placed the dead white disc on my bench. It might be satisfying to open it up later, but hardware jailbreaking an Aspis with the tools I had was pretty much like trying to edit DNA with actual full-sized scissors.

I unwrapped the new Aspis, took in one breath of Aspisless freedom, and stuck it on my arm. Its LED blinked, it booted up and connected to my Aspis account. I felt a little tingling as it applied whatever patches it thought my immune system needed. I waited for a couple of minutes until everything was working.

Then I switched on my Senselet and the oncosense, paired them with the Aspis, and opened the data feed.

For a moment, the oncosense was back. Awareness of cancer risk was a tension between my shoulder blades, bugs on my skin. But the dashboard only showed the usual suspects, osteosarcoma and friends, no sign of the Heffalump. That was good, maybe it *was* a cyst that had nothing to do with cancer—

And then the oncosense cut off again.

I searched for the weird repetitive sequences. Sure enough, they were there, like before. There was no way for two Aspises fail on me in a row.

The sequences had to be real, and somehow they stopped the Aspis from talking to the Senselet.

A suspicion began to dawn in my mind. I asked Donnie to look for Darkome posts involving Aspis jailbreaking using weird DNA sequences. There was a whole subDarkome called *aspis-jailbreak* with over eighty thousand users, which I had never seen before – but it had mainly been active when Aspises originally came out a decade ago. User BioBender speculated that an Aspis could be jailbroken using an old trick from the 2020s, when a research group had carried out a memory injection attack on an Illumina-style DNA sequencer – crafting a DNA sequence that actually contained instructions to the sequencer's *software*, letting the group take over the sequencer remotely. No one had actually managed it for Aspis, though.

I picked up my old Aspis and weighed it in my hand. Fireworks were going off in my head. It made perfect sense. I was a unique system: a Li-Fraumeni patient in an Aspis-powered cancer prevention trial. Due to my missing p53, my cancer cells had the ability to hypermutate. I remembered an old book Mom had made me read, *The Emperor of All Maladies*. Cancer cells were our dark twins, it had said, malevolent but superior versions of ourselves. Better at everything we did, better at surviving, growing.

And evolving.

Was it possible that, through countless iterations, the Heffalump had figured out how to hack the Aspis?

My heart hammered. It was a wild fantasy. Tens of thousands of Darkome hackers – and probably a smaller but technically superior number of Chinese and Russian government-sponsored hackers – had been unable to crack the chip.

But the human immune system was orders of magnitude more complex than an Aspis, and late-stage cancer still hacked it successfully. A whisper to Donnie gave me the numbers. If you treated each biochemical reaction in a cell as a floating-point operation equivalent, a tumour the size of the Heffalump was easily more powerful than any super-computer in existence.

I probed the tiny node under my arm with a finger. I needed to know exactly what the Heffalump was made of and sequence every bit of its DNA. And if there was even a slight chance that my suspicion was true, there was no one else I could trust to do it, certainly not Dr Nguyen. Maybe this would turn out to be a false miracle, too. But at least I would do the experiment to find out with my own hands.

Unfortunately, the experiment was going to involve stabbing myself in the chest with a very sharp needle.

*

I told Donnie what I was planning, and it filled out the deep tissue biopsy protocol, complete with AR tutorials, and checked the steps against my equipment list. I had a 23-gauge hollow needle that should do the job, and a serviceable MinION 2 sequencer. The only missing pieces were Proteinase K, a reagent you used to clean the tumour DNA from any protein gunk that stuck to it, and an imaging system to guide the needle to the target.

The reagent part was easy. I had a bunch of Darkome tokens left. I wasn't exactly a massive contributor to other projects – but I was now the maintainer of Mom's Li-Fraumeni project. Her death had been big news on Darkome, and it had attracted a bunch of donations. I had spent a chunk of them while trying to figure out what had gone wrong with Mom's final p53 prep, but I had enough for the odd reagent sharing request, especially one as basic as this one.

I posted a request on the BioNet subDarkome with a generous offer. I'd probably have to be patient, though, even if somebody had the reagent handy. The physical Darkome layer, a spiderweb of dead drops and anonymous drones, had limited capacity, but sometimes you got lucky.

That left the imaging. I checked Amazon for smartglasses ultrasound attachments – surely I could get one delivered within the hour. Shockingly, only used models were available, and the cheapest one started at a thousand dollars, roughly ten times what I could currently afford. It was absurd: ultrasound was eighties technology. But it was also a branch of the tech tree that Aspis had made obsolete by subsuming practically all biosensors. As if I needed any more reasons to hate them.

I racked my brain for alternatives, thinking back to our

experiments in the Harbour. My memories of the days and weeks leading up to Mom's death got smudgier every time I touched them, like a wet blot of ink. But when we had injected mRNA into her spine, we had used an old GE VScan ultrasound probe, hacked to provide an Eyes-compatible AR layer.

It had to be somewhere in Mom's stuff. I was sure Dad hadn't been able to bring himself to throw anything away, had filled a U-Haul van and dumped it all into the vertical storage unit he rented in the city.

I rubbed my face with both hands and groaned.

I was going to have to talk to Dad.

7

A Pint of the Emperor's Enigma

All right, I told myself. You meet with him, tell him you have to be somewhere else and it has to be quick. It'll be fine.

In an effort to put off the inevitable, I checked my Darkome account. *Score.* The Proteinase K was going to be delivered to a dead drop somewhere in the Mission, a short bike ride away. The logistics system never gave you the exact location. It pointed you at the general area, and then the darksense guided you to where you needed to be.

I threw myself down on my beanbag, stared at the ceiling, took a deep breath and opened a messaging app. I had last answered a message from him over a year ago, when he moved to Blythe to work on the Mojave Bloom thing. We had met in person maybe three times since leaving the Harbour, usually because he had ambushed me or engineered a situation where it was hard to refuse, like having a coffee with Mom's childhood friend Tracy.

> Hi Dad, thanks for the food. You didn't have to.

Three dots blinked, almost immediately. I closed my eyes and did boxed breathing again. When I opened them, the response was there.

> Hi peixinha, of course. I'm in town every couple of weeks now. Would love to see you.

Seeing my nickname made me swallow. He was so damn good at this, hacking my emotions without even trying.

> I'm pretty busy, but have a brief window tonight. Southern Pacific Brewing at 7pm?

> You got it!!!

The message came with a Senselet attachment, a sudden high-five slap sensation. I rolled my eyes. That was trying too hard, like throwing in a random cowboy hat emoji.

> Oh one small thing, I typed. >Would you mind bringing the fob for the SoMa storage unit? I need to grab something from there.

Three dots again. Dad wasn't stupid. He knew I was only doing this because I wanted something. But he was also needy and desperate. I hated myself for exploiting that, especially when I knew I wasn't ready to forgive him, no matter how many dishes he cooked or favours he did. It didn't feel entirely fair.

> Sure thing, he typed. > Drinks are on me.

I let out the breath I had been holding and closed the app. There was a tense knot in my stomach, and getting dressed felt like an action movie lock and load montage. AeroVoyant cycling jacket with high visibility patches, yoga pants, sneakers, backpack for all the stuff I needed to bring back, a helmet. It's Dad, I told myself. It's going to be fine.

I grabbed an e-bike from the House rack outside and sped into an evening that retained some of the day's heat. It was an easy downhill ride to the Mission, past Dolores Park and along 20th Street to Southern Pacific Brewing. The brewery was in a huge converted warehouse with industrial sheet metal walls, floor-to-ceiling windows and a couple of big trees growing inside. The foliage was decorated with twinkling string lights and the wall-to-wall hum of conversation filled the space. It reminded me of the Dark Star. I'd asked Dad to meet me there because the place made me feel safe.

He was already there, of course, at a table beneath one of the trees, face illuminated by the soft fairy LEDs. He looked healthy, less chunky than I remembered, and his eyes were clear behind his dark-rimmed glasses. He wore a Mojave Bloom Initiative T-shirt, with a desert landscape that flicked into a lush garden if you looked at it from a different angle. He had let his beard grow, and it had some grey. It felt like I had leaped forward in time, into an alternative future of some kind, where everyone I knew had changed. For a moment, I missed him: and then the feeling scraped against the granite wall of my anger.

All right, I thought. Let's get this over with.

Dad looked up when I approached. He gave me a relieved smile.

'Peixinha. I wasn't sure you would actually turn up.' I could feel that field of warmth he radiated, the reason he was so good with people. I put up my shields and sat down opposite him.

'Hi, Dad,' I said. 'Here I am.' I held out a hand. 'Let's not make this into a thing. You know I'm here for the fob. Hand it over, and you'll have done the good parent thing for the whole year. No more cooking necessary. Not even Christmas presents. OK?'

'Did I get it right? The stew?'

I said nothing.

He looked sheepish. 'It was your great-grandmother Amália's recipe. I don't think I ever told you, but I had to learn to make it before your grandmother gave her blessing—'

He saw my expression and hastily put a small black fob in a keychain on the table. It bore a stylised S-themed logo.

'One drink,' he said. 'Let me buy you one drink, and I'll give it to you. Isn't that fair after what, two years?'

I looked at him, the parts of his face that were weird distorted reflections of my own, the arc of the eyebrows, the lips. Forgiveness wasn't on the table, so he had to extract these little concessions, one by one. Fine, if that's what it took.

I crossed my arms and put my elbows on the table.

'That's fair.'

'I thought we could talk for a couple of minutes. I figured you'd be in a hurry, so I ordered a beer for you.'

He pointed to a full pint glass on the table, a dark stout by the looks of it. It was definitely an olive branch. Mom and Dad had always been paranoid about my drinking, especially since the Dark Star BBQ had taken a somewhat lax approach to serving underage customers.

'Emperor's Enigma, they call it,' Dad said. 'That thing Darin brewed for you – it was an Imperial stout, too, wasn't it?'

I frowned and took a sip. It was velvety and rich, with a bittersweet finish.

'I guess it didn't occur to you to wait and ask what I wanted,' I said, to see him flinch. I wasn't disappointed.

'Point taken,' he said quietly.

I sipped the beer again. It was actually very good,

intense but very drinkable, but so rich it would take me a few minutes to comfortably finish it. Surely, Dad wasn't Machiavellian enough to have planned that. Probably not. Probably.

'The Mojave Bloom is going well,' he said. 'It's quite something to see grasses coming up from what used to look like dry concrete, or fog catchers like giant spiderwebs. They have me doing outreach now in high schools and colleges. Young people respond to it. They want something to do, something meaningful. This girl came to me and said until I came to her school, her plan was to move to Iowa, sell her attention data for Illusia credits and that was it. It's—'

'I get it, Dad.' I took off my cycling helmet and placed it on the table. 'You don't have to sell it to me. Fixing the desert is good. But it's not my thing.'

'There's a lot of biology in it, you know. Enhanced soil microbes, engineered trees. It's—'

'Dad. Seriously. You *really* don't get to re-engineer my life any more. I mean it.' I took a long gulp of the Emperor's Enigma, then set it down. 'Half a pint to go.'

He looked at his own drink, both hands on the table. Familiar tattoos on his bare arms I'd traced with my fingers when I was a toddler: Winnie the Pooh characters on one arm, sailboats and waves on the other. I waited for the usual arguments, how he had always done what was best for me, how protecting me was the only thing he could imagine doing after Mom's death.

'I understand,' he said instead. 'Anyway, that isn't what I really wanted to talk to you about. It happened a few months ago, but I wanted to tell you in person. I met someone.'

I stared at him blankly. 'Someone?'

'Her name is Kamala. She works on project co-ordination in Blythe. She's a widower, too. We are thinking of moving in together.' He took a deep breath and folded his hands. 'Inara, I'd love for you to meet her.'

It was like a drill had broken through to some dark reservoir that gushed its contents out. I did not have a name for the black feeling that welled up in my chest. I wanted to scream.

I pushed my chair back and stood up. 'Well, that's great, Dad. That's really great.' I grabbed the key fob from the table and held it up to him. 'This. This is all I wanted, OK? I don't need to know how you are doing. I don't *want* to know. I'm *so* glad you are with someone you care about, after you made so damn sure I couldn't be.'

'Inara, we've talked about this—'

'Sure. But you never really understood, did you? What it's like to be a fucking freak. To wait for scans and hold your breath. Until maybe, just maybe, you see a way out. And then it's taken away. No. It's too easy for you. Deserts and flowers and food and *meaning*. Fuck you, Dad. Do me a favour. Go to the desert and don't come back.'

I gulped the rest of the stout down so fast it went into my nose and ran down my face, but I didn't care. Then I slammed the empty pint glass on the table.

This time, Dad didn't flinch. He looked straight at me with that clear gaze, tears welling up.

'I do know,' he said quietly. 'I do know, Inara.'

I grabbed my helmet and ran, squeezing the key fob in my other hand, bumping into people. The white noise of the brewery drowned out whatever Dad said next.

My face was wet, but I figured it was only the beer.

8

Dead Drops and Old Things

I biked uphill, hardly using the electric assist. I channelled
my anger into the pedals and the whirr of the spokes so I
could focus on the darksense pulsing in my wrist, guiding
me towards the dead drop. Warmer, colder, warmer, warmer
– and then I swerved onto a quiet narrow street, lined with
old murals. Proud African warriors, two-gun robots, sexy
motorcyclists, Frida Kahlo and roses against a green background, all weathered and chipped and sad in the orange
glow of streetlights.

I braked to a halt with a rubbery screech and wiped sweat
from my eyes. My heart still pounded, and I forced myself
to do boxed breathing again until I felt calmer and could
take a look around. The hum of the darksense helped. It
made me feel somewhat at home: you could only live and
breathe Darkome in places like the Harbour, but really, it
was everywhere, hidden in plain sight, like the mycelium
beneath a forest, secret channels of information and energy.

There was a Little Library box on a wooden pole in front
of Frida, nestled among overgrown flowers on the sidewalk.
It was in incongruously good shape, painted bright purple

with drawings of spaceships and submarines, an assortment of books behind a glass door. I rolled my eyes at the obviousness and approached it. The darksense achieved fever pitch. I opened the box and leafed through the volumes. There was a doorstopper copy of David Foster Wallace's *Infinite Jest* that looked out of place among the self-help, military history and spirituality books. I picked it up and opened it. It was hollow. Inside, a small plastic snap cap tube was sandwiched between two flat packs of dry ice. A Sharpie-written label said PROTEINASE K alongside a QR code sticker. I put on my Eyes, eyeclicked the QR code link to confirm pickup and transfer tokens, and stashed the reagent in my backpack.

One down, one to go. I felt the storage locker fob in one of my jacket's zippered pockets, and got back on the bike.

I could have sworn the street was empty, but something moved in the corner of my eye. A lump of ice materialised in my belly. I had been careless: I hadn't scoped the dead drop beforehand, or activated any countermeasures.

'Shit shit shit,' I whispered under my breath. I pulled the cycling jacket's hood over my helmet and eyeclicked my way furiously to the glasses' opsec menu. One blink, and anti-facial recognition infrared LEDs lit up in their frames. Another, and a drone detector layer descended into my field of vision.

And there it was: a twelve-inch quadcopter, hovering behind a low-hanging branch of a magnolia tree thirty feet away, its outline highlighted in white, its controller RF pulsing next to it. Standard police drone frequency. *Fuck.* There had been reports on subDarkomes of the police cracking down on dead drops recently, gearing up for a war on biohacking even before the Zephyra Lux Act passed. I had screwed up.

I got on my bike carefully, trying not to panic. The drone didn't know I had spotted it yet. The alley was dark, but it had pretty decent video of me now – still, if I was lucky, my face was not visible from that distance.

My hands shook on the handlebars a bit. I started cycling down 26th Street, glancing at the drone detector app's little radar screen in the corner of my eye.

Sure enough, it was following me.

Scenes of being arrested and handcuffed flashed through my mind, but I shut them down and focused on the road ahead. It was relatively quiet. I passed a few self-drives, a wine shop, then Victorian-style homes mixed with modern apartment buildings. It smelled of flowers and Mexican food. I could keep cycling to buy myself time to think – or I could try to lose the drone. I knew the area pretty well: one of my BarkButler clients, a high-energy greyhound called Apollo, lived around here. I needed more greenery, nooks and crannies where I could do something to change my appearance. I thought back to runs with Apollo, trying to find the fastest routes to the dog play areas in Dolores Park or Corona Heights.

I spotted a lime-coloured laundromat ahead on the right, and suddenly I had it. The drone was keeping a respectful distance. I took a hard turn right to Guerrero Street – and then immediately right again at a tree with a lush foliage. I darted into Juri Commons, a long narrow community garden hidden between two buildings, with a small playground in the middle. At this time of day, close to 8 p.m., it was completely empty.

Close to the playground there was a park bench that almost disappeared behind two large bushes. I ducked behind them, lowered the bike to the ground and tried to catch my breath. The detector app showed the drone's projected trajectory happily heading along Guerrero. A random Darkome user accessing a dead drop didn't really warrant a multi-platform manhunt. But I didn't want to take any chances.

I inverted my jacket – it had bright yellow high visibility lining – and stashed my helmet in my backpack. Then I turned the anti-facial recognition lights in my glasses off and cycled to the end of the Commons. I turned right to San Jose Avenue and backtracked to the 26th. Cycling was easy, even without the e-assist: I felt light, strong and alive, lungs full of evening air. It was as if I hadn't merely evaded the drone, but shaken off the black beast Dad had woken.

I let the wind catch my hair, turned the electric motor on and whizzed along Folsom Street, towards SoMa and all the things that were left from our lost years in the Harbour.

The ride to SoMa SkyVault Storage took around fifteen minutes. The SoMa neighbourhood had once been SF's tech hub, but now the offices and co-working spaces stood mostly empty. These days, the cool place to be was Mission Bay, around Aspis's sleek headquarters. But SoMa had its charms: actual non-pretentious art galleries and cafés, older long-term residents. And, of course, repurposed eyesores like SkyVault: an absurd glass and steel monolith that seemed to be made of the night sky. The upper levels formed a kind of lopsided staircase that made the high-rise look like the end state of a giant Tetris game. The luxury apartments it had been built to house hadn't survived the Decade of Plagues – handy for us little people who needed a place to keep our stuff.

I locked my bike in a rack and made my way to the entrance. I held up the fob, and the glass doors opened to a minimalistic, well-lit lobby. It was eerily empty, except for a middle-aged mom trying to comfort a small crying child in a pram. I headed straight to the big touchscreen wall. It would have been a pain to get my jailbroken glasses talking to the SkyVault app I was supposed to have installed, so it was easier to stay old school.

I tapped my way to the 'Access Storage Unit' option, then swiped my way through the 3D scans of all our boxes. I was pretty sure it was in a box Mom had labelled with a Sharpie-drawn infinity symbol, but I tapped a couple of other likely ones to be sure. I had all night, in any case, supposing I'd got it wrong.

I waved the key fob again, and got directions to a storage retrieval bay. That was through a set of double doors leading to a big open area. The walls there were lined with *Star Trek*-style doors with progress indicators. The ceiling panels were transparent, and I couldn't help gawking at the mirror-reflecting-mirror infinity of shelves, tracks and robotic arms above. The whole building was essentially a giant robot, the detritus of human lives its microbiome.

After a couple of minutes, the pastel doors hissed open. Incongruously, the three boxes I had picked sat on a conveyor belt, neatly stacked. I took them out. They smelled of dry cardboard and home.

The first box had my old soft toys, and another was full of old electronics cables, all tangled up in a Gordian mess.

74

That wasn't where the scanner was, but I grabbed a couple of the most ancient power cables. A visual search with my Eyes matched one of them to the VScan charging port.

I covered the cables box with the toys again and randomly picked up my old plush fish, Peixinho. We had been inseparable until I went to school. Dad had done a great high-pitched Peixinho voice. I was going to put it back, then hesitated. The little Inara in me refused to send him back into the robot labyrinth. I gave in and put the little guy in my backpack.

The box with the infinity symbol was more battered. Sure enough, the VScan was there, nested between old plastics and Mom's spiral-bound notebooks. Into the backpack it went. The acidic paper of the notebooks had already yellowed. I picked out one at random and leafed through it. It was full of notes in Mom's scrawly handwriting – she had liked to make notes on paper when she did deep thinking.

DNA kill switches, said one page. *Sequence-specific binding domains and dimerisation triggered by mutations???* There was another page on the elephant p53 protein we had pegged our hopes on, until we realised it would cause a hopelessly potent immune rejection in humans. On and on it went: Mom had had lots of ideas. I could see her writing at the small dining table of our houseboat in the Harbour, burning a scented candle that she claimed helped her think.

We could have made it work, Mom, I thought. We could have made it work. But time had run out. We had screwed up – to this day, I did not know how. But we had been close.

I closed the notebook, grabbed the others and stuffed them in my backpack as well. Something fell out from one of them. I picked it up.

It was a birthday card Dad had given Mom on her for-tieth birthday. I opened it, and it unfolded into a little paper ship. He had drawn three tiny stick figures in the cabin of the boat, and written a poem next to it.

You are the captain
You are the wind
You are the stars
Showing the way

I am the ropes
I am the sail
I am the anchor
When we finally stay

We are the boat
We are the journey
We are the new lands
Beyond the sea.

The words twisted me into a knot. There was the Dad I re-membered, the one who channelled his love through words and cooking and touching little gestures. Not the dark and sullen one, screaming out his anger, threatening the Harbour to get me signed up to PROSPERITY-A, not taking no for an answer.

What would I do if my wind died? I thought. *What would I do if the stars went out? Who would I become?*

I do know, Inara, he had said in the beer garden. And suddenly, I believed him. For a moment, I thought about messaging him, going back, saying I was sorry. Telling him that I'd love to meet his Kamala. That's what a normal person would do.

I zipped up my backpack. Dad could never find out what I was up to. He would immediately send me to Dr Nguyen, flash back into full demon Dad mode, right when it seemed like he had found some part of his old self again.

I couldn't do that to him. It was best to keep my distance. It was best for everyone.

I walked out into the cold night air. Above, the SkyVault reflected all the lights of the city, and for a second I felt like I was inside the reflection, trapped beneath the surface of a giant mirror.

Then I snapped out of it. The night was still young, and I had a Heffalump to hunt. I got on my bike and headed back down Folsom, the breeze behind my back. My jacket billowed out like a sail.

You are still the wind, Mom, I thought. You are still the captain. We will find a way.

9

Fine Needle Aspiration

I got home around 9 p.m. I was starving, so I snuck into the kitchen. Arjun was drinking herbal tea with a gangly but handsome boy who looked like a date. Arjun lifted a masseur-muscular arm and waved at me, but I didn't want to cramp his style, so I grabbed a Joylent and went to our small back garden to gulp it down.

It was peaceful back there. It smelled of jasmine, and it was nice to watch the silhouettes of my housemates move past the windows. The heat of the day had finally faded into something comfortable. I should have been exhausted, but I was full of a nervous energy, pinpoint-focused and sharp, as if I was turning into a biopsy needle myself. As soon as I finished drinking my meal replacement, I went around the house, back through the main entrance and hallway, and climbed the staircase to my room.

It took a bit of time to set things up. I cleared some space on the floor so I could lie on my back. I checked that the VScan was still working. It was, but the ancient AR layer Mom had hacked together wasn't compatible with my jail-broken Eyes. It only took a muttered prompt to Donnie to generate the code to fix it, though, and then I had handy AR windows in my field of vision that peeled back my flesh in ghostly monochrome layers.

I laid out the rest of the kit: fine-gauge needles, sterile gloves, gauze and the sample container. I had Donnie scan the room and generate a full point-of-view video of the protocol, and went through it step by step a couple of times.

It may seem obvious now, but generative AI was one of the reasons Darkome had exploded pre-Aspis. Molecular biology was a craft, you actually had to do physical stuff, a much higher bar than programming. But Donnie and his relatives could turn any protocol into a fully immersive AR experience and guide you through every step in real time. Mom had always emphasised the need to do things yourself, though. You needed that muscle memory and instincts when you were doing things that were completely new. But I didn't mind taking shortcuts for something this basic. And some handholding was helpful while I was stabbing myself in the chest.

I took off my top and lay down. The carpet was rough against my bare back. I used my right hand to press the cold rectangle of the VScan against my left breast and blinked the AR window open. And there it was, the Heffalump. A pale white blob in the grey layers of my tissue, a tiny, trapped planet.

Here comes the alien invasion, I thought, and dabbed the skin around it with an antiseptic solution using my left hand. The chill of the evaporating liquid made me shiver. I put on sterile gloves. It was awkward to hold the needle with my left hand while holding the VScan with my right, but in spite of my pounding heart, my hands were steady.

I placed the tip of the needle on my skin and pushed. There was a brief, sharp pain, and then it slid right in, a sharp wedge in the zoomed ultrasound image. Very carefully, holding my breath, millimetre by millimetre, I pushed the needle into the Heffalump.

Then came the aspiration part. I moved the needle tip around to collect cells in its hollow tip. That felt like a continuous bee sting. I gritted my teeth, my hand jerked slightly, and a lightning bolt of pain made me see black stars for a second.

Then it was done. I pulled the needle out and carefully scraped the tiny flecks of pink tissue in the tip into a container. The mark left by the needle bled a tiny crimson tear. I covered it with a bit of gauze and sealed the bandage with tape.

The adrenaline crash left me lying on the floor for a few minutes, but I didn't want to risk the sample going bad. I forced myself to do a couple of push-ups and squats, and got to work. With the Proteinase K completing my DNA extraction kit, processing the sample took only half an hour. By midnight I had a sequencing run going. I could have viewed the sequences in real time, but by this point my temples pulsed with a fatigue headache.

I stumbled downstairs to the bathroom and brushed my teeth. I passed Arjun's bedroom on my way back. Judging by the thumps and groans coming from within, his date had been successful. I felt empty, like the aspiration had pulled out all emotion along with the Heffalump cells. I didn't even have the energy to be jealous.

I put on Mom's old Captain America T-shirt, took Peixinho from my backpack, curled up in my bed and fell asleep in minutes.

10

Mycelium Dreams

I dreamed about the mycelium. It was Holst who had told me about it in the Harbour: how fungi formed these vast networks beneath forests, connecting trees to each other, mediating flows of information and energy, sending out electric pulses along long tendrils like neurons.

We walked together in the Point Pinole Regional Park. Holst was sampling the soil.

'We need a human mycelium,' he said. 'We're too alone, too disconnected. It wants to talk to us, too, and it's been trying.'

'Through magic mushrooms?' I asked and laughed. I was fifteen: a psychedelic experiment would send Dad up the wall.

'Yes. Imagine a deer, a million years ago. It eats a mushroom. The mushroom contains subtle chemicals that makes it bolder, more creative, more prone to taking risks. It wanders off its territory, somewhere new. The mushroom's spores spread to the new territory. It connects to the existing mycelium. It spreads, it connects. By talking to other creatures, showing them what they can be, connecting them.

'We are finally getting ready to talk back.' He was injecting mRNA into the ground, trying electrical impulses, planting MinIONs into the soil to map the mycelium flows. In spite of a burst of popularity before the Decade of Plagues, it had been a fringe field, and still was.

The dream flowed from the memory into something more surreal, and I was shrinking, injected into the mycelium myself, into a vast network that extended not only between trees and other beings but in time, too, into the past, into the future.

The flow took me into the deep future; the glowing lights that were the root systems of trees became stars. There were flows between them, too, diaphanous currents through the interstellar medium, made of trillions of tiny motes, each smaller than a cell. I realised they *were* cells, adapted to their new environment, able to catch laser beams and starlight for energy and propulsion, each carrying a supercoiled macromolecule that was a denser descendant of DNA, holding all that had gone before within, a history of humanity, my Darkome posts, my thoughts.

It *was* Darkome, I realised, this thing that now provided a metabiological mycelium for what humanity had become, transporting information and energy from star system to star system: entire ecosystems, countless species, packaged in DNA, ready to bloom in fertile soil. And minds, the future descendants of humans and AI fused, encoded in those coiled molecules.

I grew bigger, until I couldn't fit into the galaxy any more. I stood in the void outside it, watching the entwined flows: the stars they touched pulsed and changed, sometimes dimming as shells grew around them, sometimes brightening as they moved, propelling themselves with their own light, reflected from crystalline paraboloids in their orbits. The Milky Way was a stellar forest, vibrant and alive. Or perhaps a single slow mind whose thoughts were made up of dancing stars. I could not tell. Maybe there was no difference.

My dream-self, standing outside this fragile thing, was deeply jealous that I could not touch it. A part of me knew that in this future Darkome, you were never alone: you were always connected to other beings, were a *part* of things larger than yourself; and if you didn't like what you were, you could keep changing and growing, swapping out parts like Theseus's ship, until you became something else entirely.

In the dream, the star-giant that I was started crying. My tears fell towards the spiderweb of the Darkome galaxy, raining on the fragile flows, and I reached out to catch them so the beautiful thing that had grown out of humanity would not be drowned and shattered—

I woke up, confused and muddled. My face was wet. I sat bolt upright, and I started rummaging in my pile of clothes for the BarkButler uniform, until my brain was awake enough to catch up with yesterday's events. It was seven in the morning. The morning fog the locals called Karl rolled down the slopes of Twin Peaks outside. I needed coffee, but the sequencing data couldn't wait. I sat down at my bench in my T-shirt and undies and put my Eyes on.

I had been bracing for bad news, but my mouth still went dry as I scanned through the clustered annotations and the explanations that Donnie popped up around them.

The Heffalump was definitely an aggressive breast

cancer. It overexpressed a ton of immunosuppressive and growth-enhancing genes. It was also heavily mutated. That wasn't surprising – but in addition to the usual driver mutations, it had more of the weird repetitive sequences, long inserts that were completely unknown to the sum of biological knowledge stored inside Donnie.

And somehow they made the Heffalump invisible to the Aspis.

I stared at them until my no-coffee headache started to make itself known, pulled on yoga pants and made my way to the kitchen, still wearing Eyes. Svetlana was there, sweaty from a run, in sci-fi sleek sports gear that left her arms bare. Her Aspis was a high-end model, more like a piece of jewellery, the colour of lapis lazuli. She was making a smoothie. She raised her eyebrows when she saw me. I nodded at her, took out my Aeropress from my cupboard and started making coffee while continuing the analysis.

'Hey, Reyes,' Svetlana said.

'Hmm?' I filled the kettle and turned it on.

'You're up early. No gigs today?'

I was still thinking about the sequences, and how they worked. A nanopore sequencer pulled a strand of DNA through a tiny hole. Each DNA base pair – A, T, C, G – created a different kind of electrical signal when it went through. A machine-learning algorithm interpreted the signal.

'Oh, I got fired,' I said absently, then bit my tongue. It definitely wasn't something I wanted to get back to Thanh. I appreciated Svetlana's sudden interest in my life beyond bathroom use, but could she not display it when I was in the middle of something this important?

'Crap,' she said. 'That sucks.'

The kettle started boiling and gave me another couple of conversation-free seconds. I used the reverse-Aeropress technique for making coffee and filled half of the main cylinder with hot water, stirring the ground coffee in with a spoon.

'Yeah,' I said, and started pouring in the rest of the water. I visualised a strand of DNA with parts folding into itself, like a Loch Ness monster with fins sticking up from its back, flowing through the nanopore of the sequencer, sending out weird electric signals, the neural network trying to make sense of them—

The Aeropress overflowed and I got some near-boiling water on my hand.

'Shit!' I lifted the glasses up to my forehead – too much multitasking – and grabbed some kitchen roll to tidy up.

'Are you OK?' Svetlana asked.

I took a deep breath. My mind was racing, but my hand was also burning, and I put it under the tap. 'Sorry. I'm fine. Lots going on.'

'I can see that.'

I looked at her. This was the longest conversation I had ever had with Svetlana.

'Don't worry,' I said and closed the tap. The burn on my hand still stung like hell. 'I'll find something.'

'Let me see that.' Svetlana opened the drawer where Thanh had stashed an old first aid kit. 'Put it back under the tap and keep it there for at least another three to four minutes.'

'Yes, ma'am,' I said, surprised.

'I didn't pop out of my mom's womb as a sommelier, you

know,' she said. 'There was a time I wanted to be a nurse.' She had gauze and antiseptic cream ready, and she leaned on the counter next to me, watching my hand under the tap carefully.

'Are you going to be OK?' she asked. 'Job-wise, I mean?'

I shrugged. 'I'll find something.'

She turned the tap off. 'That should do it.' Gently, but firmly, she took my hand, dried it with a towel, applied the cream and wrapped the gauze around my hand. 'Keep changing it for a couple of days and it'll be fine.'

'Thanks,' I said, feeling strangely warm. It had been a while since someone had taken care of me like that. For a moment, I considered telling her about Heffalump, sharing the burden with someone else. Then I pulled my hand away and massaged it. Svetlana had her own problems, and it was a stretch to jump from bathroom disputes to breast cancer diagnosis emotional support.

'Don't mention it,' she said. The blender's noise made further conversation impossible for a moment, and I used it to press the Aeropress's piston down – there was still enough to make a cup – being extra careful this time. I grabbed my cup, but as I was on my way out, Svetlana turned back to me.

'How do you feel about LARPs?' she asked.

'Uh ... indifferent?'

'I have a client who runs them. They're always hiring extras. You might not need to do much except stand around and stare, and you get the script in your Eyes.' She gave me a microsecond smile. 'Thought that might be something up your alley.'

OK, so she wasn't all warmth and cuddles. But maybe I deserved the neg.

'I'll think about it,' I said.

'Let me know.' She raised a finger. 'And keep that bandage on.'

'I will. It'll be hard to clean the bathroom with it, though.'

Svetlana guffawed into her green smoothie and waved me away. It occurred to me that the oncosense me had been a bad judge of character. But now it was time to find out what the new me, the Heffalump part anyway, was really made of.

Back in my room, I told Donnie to compare the Heffalump biopsy data to the Aspis sequencer's data feed. As expected, except for the ones that had shut off my oncosense, the Heffalump transcripts were nowhere to be found.

I felt the thing on my breast. Did it feel a tiny bit bigger or was that my imagination?

'You are a clever little bastard, aren't you?' I whispered. The conclusion that was dawning in my mind was one of those things that is so big you can't see it properly when you are up close.

The miracle was real. The Heffalump had figured out how to make adversarial DNA strands that tricked the Aspis sequencer's neural networks. It had other sequences that actually gave the sequencer instructions – for example, to stop it from sending data to other devices.

I could copy those sequences.

I could use them.

The implications exploded in my head in all directions like the mycelium in my dream.

I could make mRNA that was invisible to Aspis. Hell, if I was a black hat, I could make a *virus* that was invisible to Aspis. I could try to fix my mutation without having to worry about Aspis interfering. But there was that 2020s paper I had found on Darkome forums, by the scientists who had hacked a DNA sequencer with actual DNA. They had gone further than invisible sequences.

They had actually gained full control over the sequencer.

I imagined a fully jailbroken Aspis that could make any mRNA I wanted, not only FDA-approved immune system updates, but anything. p53. Klotho to boost my cognition. No more clumsy, failure-prone IVT protocols to make self-injected mRNA. It would give me root access to my body.

I would be whole. Mallory and Holst and Jerome and the rest of the Harbour would love it.

I could finally go home.

The shout came before I could stop it. I threw my arms up and my head back and let it out. It was a long WOOOOOOOOOOO at the top of my voice, and went on until my lungs were empty. I breathed in and did it again, and again.

It wasn't until Arjun banged on my door that it occurred to me that to make this work, I also had to figure out how not to die from cancer.

11

Amanda Shah Drinks a Glass of Water

A week later, I was ready to launch project *aspis-offleash* on Darkome.

The late morning sun through my window was painfully bright. I took off my Eyes, stood up from the bench and stretched. The grind session had been epic, and I was exhausted. I was tempted to eyeclick 'publish' and collapse, but Aspis CEO Amanda Shah's Zephyra Lux Act testimonial was about to start. I had decided to launch right after it and ride the anti-Aspis sentiment on Darkome she would undoubtedly trigger.

I quaffed a mouthful of cold brew coffee and threw myself onto my beanbag. I was about to tune in to the vircast when there was a knock on the door.

It was Thanh. Her breathtaking eyes were serious. She was wearing a bathrobe, evidently getting ready for a client. What I could see of her face was puffy, and I wondered if she was in the process of adjusting her appearance. It occurred to me she had the bone structure to look like Zephyra, and dead celebrities could be morbidly popular.

'Can I come in?' she asked.

I frowned. 'I'm kind of in the middle of something. Can this wait?'

She folded her arms.

'Sorry, Inara. It really can't.'

I sighed and stepped aside. Thanh breezed in, with a rush of flowery perfume, and looked around. My room was even messier than usual. The chaos and takeaway containers now spilled over to the lab bench side. I had only left the house to do a couple of dead drop reagent runs.

'I cleaned for you especially,' I said. If she smiled, it didn't make it into her eyes.

'Your last payment didn't come through,' she said.

I cringed. I had been too head down in my project to think about my finances, dismal as they were.

'Sorry. I'll get it to you soon, I promise.' I tried to sound convincing. I *would* pay, if the jailbreak launch went well. Darkome tokens could be converted into more mainstream crypto although not vice versa, and something this big was bound to get me more donations than I could actually use for experiments.

Thanh sighed. 'Inara, I like you. You don't cause trouble.' She motioned at the lab equipment. 'I don't even mind any of this. But you have to realise that things are different than when you moved in. Glitzers *really* want to be here now, and I need the money. If you don't have a job and regular pay, I will have to give the room to someone else. It's maths, plain and simple.'

She nudged a fast food container with a tiny slippered foot. 'How's the job search going?'

I blushed. It had to be obvious I wasn't a BarkButler any more, even if she hadn't heard it from Svetlana. That triggered a thought, and I clung to it with dear life.

'Uh, great. I think Svetlana had a lead for me.'

She held my gaze for a moment. 'Good. Talk to Svetlana. She's smart.'

'Right. Yeah. I'll see if she's around later.'

'She's around.' She brushed my shoulder gently. 'Look, I know it's not easy, starting something new. I can give you until next month. That's the way it is.'

'Thanks. Yeah. I appreciate it.'

Fuck.

Thanh waved and left. A spring wound itself tight in my gut. This was it: my last best shot at showing Dad I had been right.

I flopped back down onto the beanbag and put my Eyes on. And then I was in a Congressional hearing, watching Amanda Shah drink a glass of water.

My viewpoint floated right in front of her. She looked exactly the same as in the PROSPERITY-A video from two years ago, dark and serious – except for a deeper furrow between her eyebrows, and a black pantsuit in place of her T-shirt and North Face uniform.

She picked up the glass, lifted it part-way, then stopped like a robot, stared at it for a moment, took a drink, and set it down. There was a tiny self-satisfied smirk on her lips, like an alien who had successfully faked being a human. *Did that like a boss. They suspect nothing.*

I figured *they* were the fifty angry-looking representatives who loomed above her solitary witness table on a raised two-tier dais. The room was also full of press, and of course countless virtual viewpoints like mine. I was grudgingly impressed by the way Shah bore the scrutiny with Zen-like calm.

'Would you like me to repeat the question, Dr Shah? Could you please tell the Committee why Zephyra Lux died?' That was Congresswoman Hernandez, the Committee chair. Young and angry, with a shaven head and the build of the Marine she had once been. *Republican, children's rights, gov overreach,* flashed Donnie's annotation in my Eyes.

I glanced at the AI summary of what I had missed. Not much – a couple of completely idiotic questions from the far right. *Can you provide evidence that these chips won't interfere with the religious beliefs or practices of American citizens?* I had tuned in just in time. I almost felt sympathy for Shah for having to deal with that kind of nonsense. Fortunately, she fixed that for me with her next answer.

'Madam Chairwoman. Miss Lux died as a result of a self-experiment that went tragically wrong. Her self-administered intrathecal injection of mRNA formulation that was designed to upregulate excitatory glutamate receptors in mirror neurons—'

Shah realised she'd lost 99 per cent of her audience and cleared her throat. 'Let me rephrase that. A live performer, Miss Lux was outspoken about finding an edge to compete with Illusia and other generative AI entertainment platforms. It seems her goal was to artificially enhance her sense of empathy for her audiences. To achieve this, she obtained a non-GMP manufactured, non-FDA approved mRNA drug from the illicit "biohacking" platform called Darkome.'

I could hear the quotes around the word *biohacking* and gritted my teeth. She had no idea what the "illicit platform" was capable of. She had never heard of ChoroidPlexus's

PTSD vaccine – dealing with trauma with the help of your immune system – that had helped hundreds of thousands in Darkome communities heal the scars left by the Decade of Plagues. By dismissing Darkome, she handwaved away projects like shinigami-eyes, hydrolysis enzymes expressed in the eye that could break down tear gas and had allowed environmental protestors to stand up to police brutality in the Philippines. Or HSPRescue, a mRNA drug for getting your body to produce heat shock proteins to help you survive wet bulb heat waves, which every villager in Punjab and West Bengal now stashed in their house.

Of course, if you had an Aspis, none of that worked for you.

At the same time, I wanted her to keep going. *Come on, Shah. Make all of Darkome angry so I can give them a stick to hit you with.*

Shah continued. 'Due to a faulty design, the drug triggered an autoimmune reaction against the cargo protein.' She took in a few blank stares and coughed. 'Like a peanut allergy, but in her brain. It resulted in paralysis and death within minutes.'

Hernandez leaned forward. 'So her death was not caused by her Aspis?'

'Absolutely not. It was caused by an adverse reaction to an illegal drug she self-administered without medical supervision. In fact, Miss Lux's Aspis detected the foreign mRNA and inflammatory biomarkers in her bloodstream and alerted emergency services. Unfortunately, the reaction was very acute and they arrived too late to save her life. But this is why we at Aspis have been very supportive of the Act that this Committee has been working on so tirelessly. We can provide the tools to detect and prevent such biohacking-caused harm.'

Yahtzee. That's what I wanted to hear. The live sub-Darkome feed for the hearing filled with paranoia.

> *That's it. They're going to come after us. This is exactly what DzoGene predicted.*

> *ZEPHYRA WAS A FALSE FLAG HIT THE BASTARDS*

> *OK I think we are seeing MIND CONTROL here, they have been delivering optogenetics payloads into the sheeples' brains all along and the starlink network is beaming down*

> *We need to start the protocol 2.0 rollout RIGHT NOW —*

I made *aspis-offleash* live. Almost immediately, a couple of microtokens appeared in the project's tip jar. It wouldn't get me more than a pipette head, but it was a start. In an eyeclick trance, I posted the link into as many subDarkomes as I could, while Shah droned on in the background. I was catching the wave, I could taste it. Images of a fully jailbroken Aspis flashed in my head. Maybe this was going to be the moment when the star-Darkome of my dream truly began—

I snapped out of it when the bulldog-like Representative Green barked a question at Shah.

'And why is it, Dr Shah, that Aspis has consistently refused to work with DARPA and the DoD on providing our warfighters with biological enhancements beyond basic biosecurity? Why not pursue applications like wound healing, increased strength, enhanced perception—'

I thought about my Darkome bookmark folder called SUPER-SOLDIER SERUM. It was my human enhancement wish list of genes, for the day when I could make mRNA reliably and safely and deliver it to any cell I wanted.

I grinned. If Shah kept pissing Darkome off, that day was about to arrive.

'Aspis is a shield, not a sword,' Shah said. 'Every day, it protects Americans and people all around the world. That is why we can be together in this room without fearing illness. The Aspis immune-computer interface is a powerful deterrent against any bad actor developing biothreats.

'But we are not done. We also want to protect against the biggest killers that remain. Cancer. Neurodegeneration. Old age. That's why we have been running trials like PROSPERITY-A and ABUNDANCE-A, with compelling results.'

I didn't like where this was going. All of Darkome's attention was on Shah now.

'What I am about to say has not been made public before, but is clearly relevant to the concerns of this Committee. We have been working closely with the FDA towards a new accelerated approval pathway for the Aspis platform, modelled after FDA's AAVPA platform approval in 2028, which for the first time allowed gene therapy developers to leverage safety data from previously approved AAV viral vector products. At the same time, we are launching a platform we call the Panacea Store. It will open up Aspis's capabilities – *with* the appropriate safety measures in place – to third party developers.'

There was a hush in the room. The Darkome feed exploded. I switched it to full Donnie summary mode to stay sane.

> *No way. The FDA can't be that stupid. It doesn't make any biological sense, how are they going to standardise release assays—*

> *Do the math this is going to be a ten trillion dollar company now they are going to own everyone*

> *Wow is Shah actually talking about opening up the Aspis APIs here, this is like OpenAI finally releasing weights in 2028 people—*

A pit yawned in my stomach. I could not have chosen a worse moment to launch an Aspis jailbreak project.

'From now on, to develop a new drug, you merely need to design the relevant mRNA sequence, show its safety in animal models – or, better yet, in our VivoCloud – and use the Aspis network to recruit and run clinical trials,' Shah continued. 'Drug development used to be harder than sending a human to the Moon. It will become as easy as building an app. You only need Eyes and an Internet connection.'

I dug at the implications through the layers of corporate bullshit. Could I ... use Panacea to develop my own p53 drug? Finish what Mom and I had started, but without having to hide in the shadows?

What if Shah was actually one of the good guys?

'Panacea will also discourage dangerous self-experimentation, especially for rare conditions. More importantly, modelling by both the RAND Corporation and McKinsey and Company indicates that the Panacea Store has the potential to reduce healthcare spending by 50 per cent by 2050. That is five trillion dollars. Five *trillion.*

'Those with vested interests in the entrenched pharmaceutical industry may resist this shift. To them, I say, think about why you got into medicine in the first place. Think about the patients.'

Congressman Jake Kim raised a hand. He had a sharp suit and an expensive haircut that reminded me of Svetlana's.

Moderate Democrat. Policy wonk, economic growth, long-ter-mism, supplied Donnie.

'Dr Shah,' Kim said. 'Let me remind you that the purpose of this hearing is *not* for you to pitch your company. We are here to hear your expert testimony regarding the relevance of the Aspis technology to the Zephyra Lux Act.'

Shah nodded meekly. 'I understand.'

'Even if your platform discourages harmful biohacking,' Kim continued, 'aren't you essentially asking us to put America's health in the hands of a single company? Wouldn't that make Aspis, you know, the biggest monopoly of all time? And you, Dr Shah, the chief arbiter of what it means to be human?'

'Hell yeah!' I exclaimed. Then I saw Kim's cat-with-cream smile. They were allies, I realised. He was teeing her up.

'Congressman,' Shah said. 'First, Aspis does not influence the FDA or its rulings in any way. Second, mRNA chips – or immune-computer interfaces, as we prefer to call them – are developed by several other companies, including Moderna, Novartis-Roche and BioGenesis. We are drafting a shared set of regulatory mRNA standards together with these teams to speed their medicines to the market as well. Competition fosters innovation, and we all want the best possible outcomes for *all* patients.'

Her voice became softer. 'And that is really at the heart of this. Fundamentally, we are trying to make healthcare more accessible to not only all Americans, but *everyone.* You probably know my parents grew up in India. What you may not know is that my aunt Roshni suffered from a disease called familial dysautonomia. It's a terrible condition. She had learning disabilities, dizziness and high blood pressure, frequent bone fractures and a host of other issues. I only met her once when I was a little girl. She was twenty-six. She died a year later.

'There are gene therapies under development for familial dysautonomia, but they will be extremely expensive. Many people in India will not be able to access them. They are therefore incentivised to turn to unsafe platforms like Darkome. My vision for the Panacea Store is universal access to advanced therapies. Even for the rarest of conditions. Even for people like Aunt Roshni. Safely.'

Shah had them now, and she knew it. The Committee shifted in their velvet seats. The hum of the audience became an approving murmur. She lifted her water glass, this time in a smooth motion, and drank deep.

The hearing moved on to interminable scientific expert interviews after that. I switched to following Darkome reactions and posting my *aspis-offleash* link into any thread I could.

Shah's testimony had won the bill at least some additional support. The prediction market consensus was that the Zephyra Lux Act would proceed to the next stage – committee amendments and then full chamber debate and vote – although the chance of the bill actually becoming law in its current form in the next year was only 30 per cent. That was still very uncomfortably non-zero.

But the shock of the Panacea announcement completely dwarfed legislative punditry. In parallel with Shah's remarks, Aspis had published an in-depth specification document for Panacea and an AI that explained how to use the platform and took in applications for beta access. As far as I could tell from Donnie summaries of thousands upon thousands of discussion threads, Darkome was evenly split between those who argued Panacea was yet another Aspis ploy to take over the world, and those who actually wanted to start building projects on top of it.

I wanted to scream. I had an infinitely superior alternative – a path to a full Aspis jailbreak, with none of Panacea's numerous restrictions. But no one had noticed or cared, and my megaphone simply wasn't big enough to cut through the noise. The project tip jar remained almost empty.

I probed at the Heffalump nub again. It *did* feel ever so slightly bigger now. Maybe this had been a mistake. Unless I got rid of the tumour soon, I was one missed cancer saving throw away from dying. I needed the Heffalump intact until I reverse engineered how it generated the Aspis-hacking sequences. Before Panacea, the risk had seemed worth it. But now – maybe I had already gone too far. The published *aspis-offleash* repo only had a single stealth sequence as an example. But if someone really wanted to, they could already use it to do bad things before Aspis rolled out a patch. That would seal the deal for the Zephyra Lux Act. I imagined the FBI raiding the Harbour, the faces of bioterror victims scrolling in newsfeeds.

I shook my head. Darkome users were better than that. Mallory had designed the key generation protocol to enforce trust: you had to physically meet up with two members who would vet you and run a PCR mutagenesis reaction before you got your own private Darkome key. There was a reason to ensure everyone shared the community's core values. Mallory had said that biology was a loaded gun, that it could save lives or end them, depending on who wielded it.

Had I just pulled the trigger? I could still unpublish the project: the decentralized digital Darkome only got backed up to the offline DNA sneakernet layer every hour or so. Do no harm, said the Hippocratic oath. I had never taken it, but could see the point.

I gazed at the unpublish button. It started pulsing gently, waiting for the eyeclick.

No. I turned away. I trusted everyone on Darkome more than Shah's propaganda. There had to be an alternative to Panacea. It wasn't a real option to someone like me. Shah might claim she was making drug development cheaper, but it was still beyond the reach of someone who could not even hold a dogwalking job.

Biotech VCs and philanthropists would take one look at me and run away screaming. In the best case scenario, if someone actually took the bet, it would take years. And ultimately, what Shah had for breakfast on the day of the Panacea Store review would determine whether my therapy ended up being deployed or not.

Could I possibly trust her to make that call?

I zoomed in to that last set of VR frames, right before Shah's glass touched her lips. The look in her eyes reminded me of Holst when he talked about the mycelium. She saw something bigger than herself, bigger than most people could imagine, and didn't dare to share that vision. She wasn't lying – microexpression detectors would have caught that – but she wasn't telling the whole truth either.

I wasn't going to let anyone decide how I lived or died, not ever again. Certainly not Amanda Shah.

12

The Rakia Experiment

I took off my Eyes and massaged my biological peepers. It was past noon. It didn't matter that I had pulled an all-nighter. There was more work to do. The jailbreak project was more important than ever, even if no one else cared.

I stared at my old Aspis on the bench. I needed more tokens and time to make it dance, and had neither. Mom and I had been incredibly productive in the Harbour. The price had been my parents' savings, and Dad playing house-husband.

But there was no world where I'd go to Dad for help. I hadn't heard from him since the night in the brewery, and that was as it should be.

OK. One thing at a time. Maybe I could find some way to break through the Darkome noise. A cool demo. Something Panacea would never allow.

My tired brain refused to spit out any ideas. I decided to visit Svetlana and ask about the LARP job, if only for appearances' sake. It was better than nothing.

I stomped down the stairs to Svetlana's door, making sure to make enough noise to be heard in Thanh's room on the third floor. I knocked and Svetlana opened the door, dressed in what I guessed passed for casual for her: designer joggers and a loose black cashmere sweater. A faint smell of roses wafted out.

'Hi,' I said.

'Reyes. How's the hand?'

I held it up. The skin was still red, but it was mostly healed. 'I can still play the violin.'

'What?' She massaged her forehead and grimaced. 'Sorry. I don't do English idiom well this hung over. Occupational hazard.'

With her near-perfect English, it was easy to forget that her native language was Bulgarian.

'Stupid joke, ignore me. Thank you for your help. Speaking of which, uh, Thanh sent me to see you. About the LARP job. I don't actually want it, but I'd really, really appreciate it if you told her I was looking into it.'

'OK,' she said. 'I will. How are you doing?'

I could see a glimpse of her room behind her. I'd imagined it would be the polar opposite of mine, all minimalism and a perfectly made bed with crisp white linen, but it was more human than that. There was a hand-woven carpet on the floor and a wooden shelf that held wine bottles, books and a delicate rose oil diffuser, which explained the rose smell.

I paused. I didn't want to pour all my troubles on her: it would be pathetic, and rose-scented or not, she had thorns.

She put her hands on her hips. 'Seriously, I'm not going to judge. I didn't patch you up so Thanh could kick you out. Let's say I need a distraction from work, a project, and you look like you could be one. What do you need?' She winced and covered her eyes. 'Anything not involving bright lights or loud sounds, that is.'

I stared at her. A cool demo, I thought. Very cool indeed.

'Uh, this is going to sound weird, but ... what should I drink if I want to get drunk? Like, really fast? And have a terrible hangover?'

'Reyes, I don't know what's going on with you, but whatever it is, getting drunk is not that helpful. It's sometimes good for a reset, don't get me wrong – worked out great last night – but it doesn't sound like that's what you are looking for.'

'No, it's ... it's for an experiment.'

She studied me with her calm blue-eyed gaze. It wasn't exactly a Haunted House secret that I messed around with Darkome. While most glitzers kept their distance from anything actually illegal, they also operated in a grey area, getting paid under the table in cash or crypto. But you never knew.

She guffawed.

'Hah. *Bozhe moy!* You've come to the right place, sister. I have rakia. Fruit brandy. It's the thing. I'll give you a bottle, on one condition.'

'What's that?'

'You're not drinking it alone.'

A couple of days later, we met on the Haunted House's rooftop. There was a parasol, a grill, a few rickety chairs and a table, although the current crew didn't use them much. Apparently the previous inhabitants had been more social. That made me think of Thanh's ultimatum. You never really stayed in the Haunted House, you moved on and left ghostly impressions behind.

Svetlana put two glasses and the colourful bottle of grape rakia on the table. She filled the glasses with the clear, sweet smelling liquid and lifted one, but I stopped her.

'Let's do one thing first. Can you record a video?'

She nodded and put her Eyes on.

I held up my electroporator. It looked like the lost love child of a taser and a syringe. Svetlana's eyes widened, but I hushed her, looked at the pulsing red dot in her Eyes' frame, and smiled.

'Do you like booze, but hate getting drunk?' I intoned, trying to sound like an old commercial. The quality of the performance didn't matter much: the video would be the seed for an AI edit that would also make me and my voice unrecognisable, keeping my RL identity separate from my Darkome one. 'I have a solution for you! FGF21 mRNA.' I flicked my fingers to add a tag to have Donnie splice a visualisation into the video from my description. 'It's a naturally occurring protein that plays a key role in your metabolism, liver health and muscle growth. As a biologic drug, it helps with weight loss. It's one of the best studied anti-ageing interventions.

'And it also keeps you sober if you drink too much, as has been well demonstrated in mouse studies.' I pointed at the table. 'Me, a nineteen-year-old female weighing a hundred and thirty pounds, is going to drink at least half of this bottle of rakia, alcohol content 60 per cent, over the next hour. I plan to be completely sober by the end of it. I'm going to do a Digit Symbol Substitution Test and the Trail Making Test to determine the impact on my cognition.

'That's going to be possible because I'm about to get my left thigh muscle to make enough FGF21 to kick my noradrenergic neurons back to sobriety in no time.'

I had burnt the few donated tokens *aspis-offleash* had netted me on a FGF21 mRNA variant incorporating the Heffalump sequence, plus an Fc domain for stability. I'd had it dead dropped in dry ice to a bin in Dolores Park. The mRNA was chemically modified, with a basic backbone, no fancy proprietary delivery tricks like Aspis used, but good enough for getting my muscle cells to make a protein that only had to be secreted into the bloodstream.

'Don't believe me? Try it yourself. Go here and download the sequence.' I held up my hand, popping a Q-glyph for my project into the video.

'Oh? You're worried about Aspis detecting something foreign and calling the cops, or doing something nasty? Well, the mRNA in here' – I tapped the electroporator – 'has a little something that *hides* it from Aspis's prying eyes.' I tapped the mRNA chip on my arm. 'And now the main event.'

The electroporator was basically a tiny taser whose electrical impulses opened up pores in the cells to make it easier for mRNA to get in. Somewhat self-consciously, I was wearing shorts. I pressed the electroporator's prongs into my left thigh – my right one had too much scar tissue from the osteosarcoma surgery – and hit the switch.

It was like being bitten by a rattlesnake, and if Svetlana had not been recording, I'd have screamed. She grew pale when she saw my expression and started to get up, but I motioned her to sit back down.

I forced my mouth into a grimace that resembled a smile, while a red flame kept burning a hole in my thigh.

'There. See you in an hour.' I'd have a timestamped set of booze-drinking photos for the *aspis-offleash* project page, before recording a second video for the Digit Symbol Substitution Test. I'd pair it all with my real-time Aspis data. It was all for show, of course, but most of it was hardware authenticated and would have taken an unreasonable amount of effort to fake – which my target audience would appreciate.

I lifted the glass. 'Here's to Zephyra.' Then I downed it in one go, bracing for another burn, but instead it had a smooth and fruity taste, refreshing in the early afternoon heat. Then I ran the edge of my palm across my neck to get Svetlana to stop the recording.

She snapped her glasses off. '*Az li sam luda, ili*—' She jumped up. 'What the hell are you doing to yourself, Reyes? Are you all right?'

I held up the glass. 'I'm fine. Fill me up.'

'I heard about that avant-garde artist girl,' she said quietly. 'Are you *sure* you're going to be fine?'

I spread my arms. 'Look, Ma, no autoimmune reactions! No FBI coming to get me either. It's working.' I didn't want to tell her my Heffalump story yet, so I explained I had come up with a stealth sequence that could hide anything from the Aspis.

'Well, I'll drink to that,' she said, eyes wide, and we did. My thigh was still pulsing with pain, and I felt a slight buzz from the alcohol. It was going to take a while for enough FGF21 to flood my system to produce an effect – I'd gone for a fast-translating mRNA construct, but I still had an hour of potential drunkenness before it really kicked in.

We drank some more. Svetlana kept staring at me like she'd never seen me before.

'That's incredible,' she said quietly. 'I wish I could do what you do.'

'Really?'

She nodded. The rakia warmed my belly, and I was suddenly happy. The day was beautiful, and I was getting drunk with a new friend.

'You said you wanted to be a nurse,' I said. 'Why didn't you go through with it?'

Svetlana took another drink. The stuff was strong, but she threw it back like it was water, even without FGF21. She looked into the distance, at Twin Peaks and the looming Sutro Tower, eyes darkening.

'My mom was a doctor,' she said. 'I grew up in a small town called Melnik, in the mountains. My dad had a small vineyard. Small community, people looked after each other. My mom delivered babies, knew everyone by first name, you know? My brother and sisters all wanted to go to Sofia to be game developers or to work in hospitality, but I wanted to study medicine and come back, do what mom did. I had already started, when I came back one Christmas break in 2035.

'What you have to understand is that we got Aspises in Bulgaria a couple of years after everyone else. The usual story, corruption, inefficiency. That was towards the tail end of the Decade, and we got hit by a Plague. A bad one. Did you ever hear about the Zmeyevit Disease?'

I shook my head. Back in the Harbour, Mallory had once given me a lecture on the weirder Plagues when I was helping her and Jerome to work on the community's DIY immune update shots, but the focus had mainly been on ones that circulated in the US. I'd never heard of Zmeyevit.

'Not sure if it made it here, or it might have had a different name. It was a two-headed beast, really. There was a virus, of course. You'd understand better how it worked, but it was the basic coronavirus backbone, you know, aerosols, infectious, basic cold symptoms, dice roll to make it really bad for some people. And somehow it gave you the Capgras syndrome.'

'The what?'

Svetlana grimaced. 'It made you think your loved ones had been replaced by impostors. Your sense of who else is a human gets messed up. You think other people are zombies, or pod people. So you don't trust anyone. That's where the name comes from. *Zmey*. A shape-shifting dragon.'

'Shit.' I could already see where this was going. I'd heard something about chaos in Europe, but it would have been around my dark osteosarcoma days. The whole Decade was a dark tapestry of stories like this, and people were still piecing it all together. 'Svetlana, that's awful.'

'Yeah.' She filled my glass. 'Keep drinking. It gets worse.'

I did as I was told. 'You said a two-headed beast. What was the other thing?'

'Bots,' Svetlana said. 'Social media bots pretending to be everyone.'

'Fuck.'

She rubbed her face with both hands. 'It's pretty clever, really. You fill the hospitals with people who don't want to be treated because they think the doctors are aliens. Government tries to stop the spread with lockdowns, so you can only talk to people online. And then you get all the bots spreading lies and pretending to be your friends, so even if you are healthy, you don't know who to trust. So then you go and meet people in person. And catch the virus.'

'Svetlana.' Maybe it was the rakia, but it felt right to reach out and take her hand. 'That's the most godawful fucking thing I've ever heard. I'm so sorry.'

She squeezed my hand back and flashed a microsecond smile.

'I can talk about it, you know. At that level. How clever it was. How neatly everything broke. They were lynching doctors in Sofia. But my village ...' She sniffed. 'That's harder to talk about.'

'It's OK. You don't have to.'

She closed her eyes and was quiet for a time. Then she looked at me, blue eyes wet. 'There was this woman, Elitsa. I'd played with her kids. Mom had delivered some of them. We were trying to give her paxlovid, it sort of worked on Zmeyevit, get her to swallow the big pills, you know? She screamed at us, called us witches. I got too close.'

Svetlana brushed back the long locks of hair that covered her right ear. It had piercings, but faintly, beneath them, I could see a scar.

'She bit my ear off. Mom got the drugs into her, but I couldn't keep going. I couldn't do anything to help them.' She smiled sadly. 'So, I didn't become a nurse. Our family never caught Zmeyevit, thankfully. We made it through. But the people in the village, it was never the same. Everybody still looking at each other like they were dragons in disguise.

'Mom burned out. My dad sold the vineyard. They moved to Sofia to live with my big sister. I needed to get away. My brother was in London, and somehow I got in to this wine school. I guess there's a reason why I like wine. It reminds me of what things were like, before. And it connects people. It's the anti-Zmeyevit.'

'I'm so sorry,' I said again, quietly. She patted my hand.

'Don't be. It's life.' She looked at me curiously. 'That's a lot of rakia you've been drinking, Reyes. Is your experiment working?'

My tongue felt thick and heavy, too. 'Not yet.'

'Good,' Svetlana said, and poured more rakia. 'Because you are going to tell me *your* story now, Inara Reyes.'

I could definitely feel the rakia now. It was like a hammer, but a *soft* hammer that didn't hurt but made everything floaty, and my words seemed to come out more easily. Come on, FGF21, please work, I thought. Do your thing.

'There is this place called the Harbour,' I said. My voice sounded like it was coming from somewhere far away. 'Have you ... have you ever been to Burning Man?'

Svetlana shook her head.

'But you've seen virs or videos, right? Desert, this giant city of makeshift buildings, cars shaped like – like—' I almost said *dragons*, but caught myself. 'Like ... fish. Crazy outfits. Parties. It's not really about that, although people go there to party, it's really about gifting. Making something cool and sharing it with others.' The thing was, I hadn't actually been to Burning Man either, but listening to Holst and Mallory, it felt like I almost had; one more for the post-jailbreak bucket list. Or maybe the Burn in my head was better than the real thing.

'I can see that means a lot to you,' Svetlana said quietly.

'Yeah. Well, not only to me. It's been going on for a long time. A couple of decades ago, these two Burners, Holst and

Mallory, wanted to create a place where all the art that got made for the playa, the desert, could be kept. They had some tech money so they bought land around a small defunct harbour in East Bay, and turned it into a Burner community. In the beginning, it was about the art, but then all the other principles crept in. Radical self-expression. Self-reliance. Sustainability.

'When they had a couple of dozen people living there, the Decade kicked off. COVID, Polarivirus-28, CEREM-V, MARV-16. They immediately got on Darkome and started making their own vaccines. Mallory might even have been one of the actual Darkome founders. They didn't like Aspis becoming the default solution, so they kept doing their own thing. Mallory was really paranoid about Aspis so they forbade anyone from using the chips in the Harbour. There's a few other places like that, here and there, more than you'd think, running entirely on Darkome, but the Harbour was one of the first and oldest.'

My voice was steadier now. Maybe the FGF21 levels in my blood were finally starting to creep up to reasonable levels. 'Sorry, one sec.' I put on my Eyes and checked. Yep. The Aspis did not have proper proteomics, but some of the correlate biomarkers like insulin were definitely behaving like they were supposed to.

'So how did you end up there?' Svetlana asked. I looked at her and rubbed the macule on my forehead. It was still hard to talk about it. But she had been open with me, trusted me, and she had lived in a place where they thought the person next to them might be a shapeshifting dragon. The least I could do was to trust her back.

111

So I told her about Li-Fraumeni, and Mom, and the Harbour, and how Dad had made me leave.

'*Strashno e!*' Svetlana said. 'That sounds awful.'

'Well, the cancer part was. But the Harbour was awesome. I was fourteen when we moved there,' I said. 'Not many kids there, old Burners and slightly younger techies, so everyone sort of adopted me, I guess. Especially Holst. I loved it. Everyone was such a weirdo. There's crazy art everywhere, giant bees and electronic temples and gramophones.'

Svetlana raised her eyebrows, her blue eyes like cool pools of water. 'Uh huh.' She rolled the bottom of her glass on the table. 'So why did you never go back? Would your dad actually do this? Smear this Harbour place with shit with the media?'

I squeezed my eyes shut.

'I don't really know him any more. I have no idea what he would do. Maybe he's in a better place now, but ... I don't know. And I'm ... I'm really scared I'll end up like Mom. I miss the Harbour, but at least I'm surviving.'

'Take it from me,' Svetlana said. 'Surviving alone is not worth it. But you have this new thing now, this ... exploit. This zero-day. If it works, you could go back, right?'

'Oh yeah. I'd be a hero. I could have my Aspis make p53, or make gene edits, or whatever I wanted. But it's not going to happen. I don't have the Darkome tokens or the money to make it work.'

'Look. I'd help you if I could, but I don't understand this stuff. Wine is complicated, but in a different way.' She ran a finger along the rim of her glass. 'But it sounds like these people, Holst, Mallory, Jerome, Darin, they really did care about you. And they are Darkome people. Have you thought about asking *them* for help?'

She grabbed my hand and squeezed hard.

'You think you let them down by leaving. But maybe they have been giving you space. If they cared about you, would they really expect you to *die* to live in this Harbour place? Especially when you were, what, seventeen when you left? If I were you, I'd give them a call.'

I blinked. Svetlana was right. Getting in touch with the Harbour founders and Jerome hadn't even occurred to me. Suddenly, I was stone cold sober, my mind completely lucid and clear.

'Holy shit,' I said.

'It worked?' Svetlana asked.

'Yeah.'

Svetlana narrowed her eyes. 'OK, cool. I can see this could be big. But be careful. It seems like a lot of people might want it.'

But all I could think about was the possibility of finally going home.

Svetlana got up and stretched. 'I'm going to go sleep this off. Got to work tonight. I'll tell Thanh you have a lead.'

'Wait.'

'What is it?'

I was about to say that we still needed to shoot the ending for my Darkome project video, but it didn't seem important any more. Instead, I gave her a warm smile. 'Thank you, Svetlana. I really mean it.'

'*Nyama problem.* Keep the bottle. And watch out for the *zmeyove.* For the dragons. I'll see you around.'

She squeezed my shoulder and headed downstairs. I took

one more sip of rakia, savouring the sweet taste with a clear head. Then I followed her and went to my room to call Jerome.

13

Reunion

Late afternoon the next day, I took a self-drive to Point Molate to meet Jerome. On the last leg of the journey, the Mordor-like towers of the Chevron refinery and the arc of the Richmond Bridge fell behind, replaced by undeveloped hills. Jerome had picked the location: the long-abandoned Point Molate Naval Depot a couple of miles from the Harbour. I had not been this close to home in two years.

The car was the cheapest I could book for the whole evening, and the air-conditioning had a glitch. I huddled in the freezing cold in my cycling jacket and Giants cap and cargo pants. I had considered dressing up, even putting on make-up, but had decided against it. Jerome was going to see me as I was. This was business, not a lovers' reunion.

Out of my Harbour friends, Jerome had been the logical choice. Especially with the Zephyra Lux Act looming. Holst and Mallory would be too careful. They'd take the idea to a community meeting and debate the ethics, maybe even post a poll on Darkome. They might decide to help in the end, but with precautions and oversight. I didn't have time for any of that, and it was better to ask for their forgiveness than permission.

Disregarding our history, the only downside to Jerome was that he had never become the major Darkome figure he had aspired to be. He had never made it to DzoGene's show – the vircast had stopped soon after I left the Harbour. After a frantic period of activity following the Kintu weights release, his public project contributions had also slowed down to a trickle. I had often wondered what had happened.

I would soon find out.

The sun dipped lower and turned the clouds amber. Point Molate was a strange place, a timeless no man's land between the Harbour and the rest of East Bay. At the heart of it was the sprawling, decommissioned Navy depot. The road hugged the shoreline and the car passed skeletal remains of fuel loading platforms and pipelines. The rusted metal frames intertwined with the overgrown foliage.

Then the car reached the depot itself. It halted in front of a concrete storage bunker, empty and silent. Tall grass peeked through the cracked asphalt of the parking lots.

I got out. The late afternoon sea breeze felt warm after the freezing ride. I could hear the waves, lapping at the decrepit piers jutting out into the water. I walked through the desolation, past the bunkers and crumbling administration buildings, the rows upon rows of suburban clone houses where the personnel had lived. My destination was Winehaven, a giant red brick structure in the middle of the depot, with castle-like turrets and fortifications.

It was surrounded by a linked wire fence, but I found the hole in it exactly where I remembered it was, next to a large palm tree. I made my way through the overgrown courtyard and into the cavernous main floor. The Navy had used it for storage, but it had once been the Bay Area's largest winery, which made me think of Svetlana. Now it was empty apart from dust and the smell of urine.

'Jerome?' I called out. My voice echoed from the high ceilings and maroon walls.

I saw a human figure from the corner of my eye, and my heart jumped – but it was only a boxing dummy, a vaguely man-shaped thing without legs, on a solid rounded base. It stood with others like it against a wall that also held cardboard cutouts of ski mask-wearing armed men. Those were peppered with bullet holes. One day, when Jerome and I had snuck in here, we'd spotted a group of Homeland Security officers training, or pretending to: drinking beer, occasionally firing their service weapons at the targets, half-heartedly punching the dummies. We'd made our way past them undetected and to the roof. We had made love there in glorious view of the whole Bay. It had been our second time.

Footsteps crunched on the debris-covered concrete floor behind me. I turned around and saw Jerome.

He wore an excursion suit – flamboyant hazmat gear some Harborians used out of an abundance of caution when leaving the village. They were fashion statements as well as practical. Jerome's outfit was black and sleek, with flaring triangular shoulder pads, comic booky glowing blue discs and circuitry in the torso, and a fishbowl helmet.

'Hey,' I said.

'Hi.' His voice came through speakers in the chest, un-naturally loud.

I crossed my arms and glowered at him. 'That's a little

extreme, don't you think? I don't have any active infections.'

'The updates are always behind,' he said. 'The Plagues are still in circulation, you know. Aspises lull you into a false sense of security.'

I frowned. 'Yeah. That's why I'm here.'

He sighed. 'I know. I'm sorry. That came out wrong.'

Jerome took a few steps closer, and now I could see his face through the faceplate properly. He was clean-shaven. The old burn scar on his cheek was gone, and he seemed a little leaner.

'You look well,' he said.

'You too.' I ran a finger along my cheek. 'What happened there?'

He shrugged. 'Decided it wasn't me any more.'

I said nothing. Being marked had been something we'd shared, once.

We stood still for a moment. Looking at him through the suit's faceplate made me feel strange, like I was a creature in an aquarium he was studying through the glass.

'How's everybody? Mallory? Holst?' I asked finally.

'You know. Good. Freaking out about the Act. Mallory is rebuilding the whole Darkome stack to get ready. Holst is trying to keep us sane and glued together. You didn't hear this from me, but he found an ex-witness protection operative to help create backup identities for *everyone*.'

'How on earth is he doing that?'

Jerome shrugged. 'It's Holst. He was probably their grandfather's psychedelic guide or something. Anyway. It's going to be a big Burning Man this year. A lot of people think it might be the last.'

'What do you think?'

'Oh, you know me. I'm a contrarian. Big changes are coming, but not in the way people think.'

'Some things don't change, though,' I said. 'You still like being mysterious.'

He gave a nearby boxing dummy a push. It wobbled back and forth. 'And you're still full of surprises. It was nice to hear from you.' The voice box amplified the tone of regret in his voice. 'I wasn't expecting to.'

'Jerome. Look.' I reached out and touched his shoulder, then drew my hand back with a yelp. The surface was scalding hot.

'Sorry, sorry, sorry,' he said, taking my hand. 'It's the cooling system, I should have warned you. Are you all right?'

I pulled my hand away, sucked on my fingers. They stung, but didn't seem to be badly burnt. 'I'm fine. And an idiot. Can't seem to learn from past mistakes.'

He smiled. 'I can relate. What are we doing here, Inara?'

'It's not about us, Jerome,' I said quietly. 'I finally have a shot at coming back. Maybe even finding a new angle for the Harbour, if the Act gets through. But I need your help.'

'Come along, then,' he said. 'Let's walk and talk.'

We did a circuit around the building and the courtyard. As the clouds started to get a tinge of red, I told him about the Heffalump and the stealth sequence. It was hard to read his reactions inside the helmet. At the same time, I was grateful for the suit. It made him less real.

When I explained my plan, he suddenly stopped.

'Inara,' he said quietly. 'This is a terrible idea.'

'Don't think of it as a terrible idea,' I said. 'Think of it as a beautiful directed evolution system. Me, the Aspis, the

Heffalump. It already cracked the sequencer, now I need to create the right conditions to crack the synthesiser as well. I know it's going to work.'

'I'm not saying it won't,' he said quietly, almost a whisper even with the voice box. 'But it's incredibly dangerous. It's an awful lot of moving parts. It could kill you in a dozen ways, Inara.'

'That's why I need your help. We can make it work. Come on. It's *not* harder than the Kintu hack you and Mallory put together, for God's sake. This *will* work. And once it does, I can get rid of the Heffalump – the tumour. It's localised. My oncologist can cut it out. After that, the p53 part is easy. I'll have the Aspis deliver gene editors and boom. I won't even need an Aspis any more.'

'I don't know, Inara. I mean, don't get me wrong, the idea is incredibly cool, but—'

'You *have* changed,' I said, suddenly furious. 'Who wanted to stay here after we spotted those Homeland guys? Or, or – when I met you, you had left home all on your own, with nothing, to work on stuff you believed in. You *inspired* me to think of this idea, Jerome Brown. I don't know what you have been doing for the past two years, but the Jerome I knew would have jumped at the chance.'

'This was a mistake, Inara,' he said. 'We shouldn't have come here.'

'Then why *did* you? And wearing that thing? I know the risks, they are not zero, but almost. It's a fucking stunt! You're saying, *Inara, you left, you're not one of us*. You are *punishing* me.'

I turned away from him, tears in my eyes. 'You're right. We shouldn't be here.'

I started walking back through the building, to the corner with the boxing dummies. For the hell of it, I took a big swing at the one Jerome had pushed. It connected with a satisfying smack. Then my wrist bent. It hurt like hell.

'Ow,' I said, and cradled my hand to my chest. It didn't seem to be broken but I really needed to stop damaging myself.

'Inara.'

It wasn't the supernaturally clear, amplified Jerome. It was his real voice, the one I remembered.

Jerome had taken off his helmet. Without the scar, he was almost too handsome, his mop of shaggy chocolate hair now loose, chiselled cheekbones that Mom had always said made him look like young Henry Golding. As I watched, he peeled off the rest of the suit and let it fall to the floor. He wore a white mesh T-shirt and joggers underneath. He looked lean and strong, with wiry rock-climber arms.

'This ... this wasn't for the Plagues,' he said, pointing at the suit. 'It was for me. I needed ... something between us. An extra layer. Do you understand?'

I looked at him and swallowed hard. 'Yeah. I do.'

He took a step closer. 'I wanted to see you. And I wanted to hear you out. But ... I can't help you with anything that is going to harm you, Inara. Ask anything else, but not that.'

'I don't *want* anything else,' I whispered. 'I want to come home.'

'You can make your home anywhere, Inara.'

'Maybe you can. But I can't.' I walked towards him, hands at my sides. 'Come on. I'm begging you. Help me.' I could smell him, sweat and an earthy cologne.

He looked down and took a deep breath.

'Inara, there's ... there is something I need to tell you. After your mom died, I ... I talked to your dad. I told him about PROSPERITY-A.'

'You did WHAT?'

'I had to, Inara. I couldn't watch you die like Manuela, not when there was a chance—'

I pushed him in the chest, hard. He stumbled backwards.

'You COWARD. Don't you DARE say her name.' The same rage that Dad held behind his cuddly exterior rose up to consume me. I punched Jerome in the face, not caring that pain exploded in my wrist. He fell backwards on his ass, clutching a bloodied lip. I stood over him, breathing hard, shaking. He rose up to one elbow. Blood flowed down his chin.

'I had to, Inara,' he said through his hand. 'I had to.'

I slumped down to my knees on the concrete next to him. But the rage wasn't done. I grabbed his flimsy T-shirt and shook him.

'I swear to God, Jerome, you are going to help me with this, or you are going to regret being born. If it kills me, it's *my* decision. My choice. I was too scared to fight last time, but not now. Not now. I am going to do this, and you – are – going – to – help – me.' I emphasised each word with an open handed slap with my good hand. Then I grabbed his face and kissed him, hard, tasting the blood. For two breaths, he kissed me back.

Then he pulled away, and I let him go.

'OK,' he said.

'What?'

'OK. I will help you. You're right. I owe you. But this' – he flicked a finger in the small space between us – 'this can't happen. Not now. If I'm going to keep you alive, it has to be cold science, professional. I'm going to build a wall, and stay behind it. Otherwise, if something happens to you, I'm going to break. Do you understand?'

Slowly, I nodded. Rage and desire played tug of war in my chest. He was right. I *had* come in with expectations. The stakes were too high for us to act the lovestruck teenagers we had once been. The anger at the betrayal helped, too. I curled my mind around it like a hand around a glass shard.

'And ... If you are right about this,' Jerome said quietly, 'it is bigger than the two of us. Bigger than the Harbour, maybe bigger than Darkome. So we need to do this right.'

I remembered my mycelium dream, star-motes and thinking suns. 'Yeah. Amanda Shah is not going to get to write the future on her own.'

We both got up. Scuffed and with blood on his face, he looked more like the Jerome I remembered.

He offered his hand. 'Partners?' He flashed his piratical grin, but his green eyes were sad like the sea.

'Partners,' I said, and we shook on it. 'Ow.' I pulled my hand away, and massaged my wrist again.

'We need to get that looked at,' he said.

I tried to smile through the pain. 'Don't worry,' I said. 'I have a friend who's good at this kind of thing.'

For a moment, we stood still again.

'OK. Funding and tokens first,' he said. 'I know someone who can help. I'm going to make some calls.'

I nodded, turned away and walked back to the car. It took all my willpower not to look back to see if he was still standing there, watching me go.

14

The Dark Angel

'That's it,' Svetlana said. 'That's the look.'

I studied myself in the mirror. The double-breasted pin-striped suit was oversized and the sleeves were too long. I liked the cocky angle of the fedora, though: it covered up my forehead macule nicely. We were in Held Over, a retro clothing store on Haight Street in the Mission. I had been trying on everything Svetlana had been throwing at me for over an hour, and I was exhausted and headachy from the smell of old clothes.

'We still need something sciencey, though,' she said, stroking her chin. 'Goggles, maybe.'

I rolled my eyes. 'No goggles.'

'You won't be able to wear Eyes in the Spliceasy anyway. Might as well have some cool eyewear.'

It was two in the afternoon three days after my meeting with Jerome. He had been quiet until the day before, which had given me a chance to make some progress with the Heffalump. Then he had BodyTimed me that we had a meeting set up with a potential backer, at the Spliceasy, a famous Darkome bar. Many Darkome joints in the city were temporary pop-up places, only findable through darksense, but some were sufficiently cool and arty that even the law turned a blind eye to them. Zephyra Lux had debuted at the Spliceasy. When I told Svetlana about the venue, she immediately insisted on helping me put an appropriate outfit together.

I tugged at my collar. 'Can we lose the tie?' I asked.

'No,' Svetlana said flatly. Even on a casual afternoon stroll like this, she was in designer jeans, a black polo and a sleek steel-grey raincoat.

'I honestly will pay you back as soon as I can.'

She looked at me, cool blue eyes unreadable, and smiled faintly. 'Don't worry, you will. But you *do* need someone looking out for you, Reyes.'

'What do you mean? Oh. Right.' I held up my bandaged wrist. Svetlana had concluded it wasn't broken, merely sprained, and had not sent me to the ER. I had considered ordering a bunch of pro-healing mRNAs via Darkome's BioNet, but was running low on tokens, and pipetting didn't hurt too much.

'There's that,' she said.

I narrowed my eyes. 'And something else?'

'It's nothing.' She held up yet another jacket, then tossed it away. 'Some kind of doctor's black bag, maybe. Or a gas mask,' she muttered.

'Tell me, Svetlana.'

'All right.' She dumped the clothes in her hands onto the booth's small bench and crossed her arms. 'I was a little surprised it was the boy you decided to see.'

'I told you. Jerome is good at hybrid bio/cyber stuff. He has the contacts. And Holst and Mallory would seriously get bogged down in committees and paranoia, respectively.'

'Uh huh,' Svetlana said. 'I'm sure that makes sense to you. In my experience, you can trust family. Exes, not so much.'

'Like I said, there's not going to be any ex stuff. Only business. And Holst and Mallory aren't family either. Mallory didn't want me in the Harbour in the first place. And Holst—' I swallowed the words. *He let me go. He didn't fight for me.*

'It's complicated,' I said aloud.

'I know,' Svetlana said. 'Families always are.' She passed me a pair of Burning Man-style brass-framed, blue-lensed goggles. 'Try these.'

I sighed and put them on. 'Perfect,' she said, and nodded. 'Remember to not take shit from anyone and you'll do great. Then we celebrate.'

I adjusted the goggles. They did go well with the fedora and made me look a little bit like a pulp hero, like Kato, The Green Hornet's martial artist chauffeur, who did all the actual fighting. I struck a karate pose.

'That's the spirit,' Svetlana said. 'But no punching.'

I lifted the goggles up to my forehead and looked at her. 'Thanks, Svetlana. You don't have to do this, you know.'

'*Sestrentse*, once you learn to know me better, you'll realise I never do anything I don't want to. Why do you think my job is getting people drunk on wine while pouring bullshit into their ears?' She patted me on the back and started rummaging through the clothes pile again. 'Now, the goggles need a slightly different shade of blue. Let's find another jacket.'

I groaned loudly at the mirror, but inside, I was smiling.

*

In spite of all the effort, I was grateful for the outfit when I saw Jerome's reaction. We met outside a nondescript apartment building in SoMa, in front of a graffiti-splattered door. Jerome was in black tie, a sort of Great-Gatsby-meets-cyberpunk look, with a bioluminescent face mask and an elaborate wire-and-gears flower in his lapel. His eyes widened slightly when he saw me.

'All right, see, the big cheese gonna dig the cut of your jib, see? Ya got the look, ya got the style, ya got the moxie, see?' he said in torturous gangster patois.

I rolled my eyes. Jerome made bad jokes when he was nervous. 'Honestly, I could have used a download on this person, Jerome,' I said. 'I don't like going into something like this blind. Also, *the big cheese?*'

'Don't worry. If you show him what you showed me, it's going to be great.' He paused. 'You'll love him. He's ... he's not the kind of person you talk about.'

I shrugged. It felt like a big exam day in school. 'Sounds like a charmer. Since when is Jerome the Great intimidated by anyone?'

He sighed. 'Not intimidated. He's helped me a lot, so I want to be sure we make a good impression.'

'Got it. Well, I trust you. You lead. I follow.'

He made a theatrical bow and opened the graffitied door for me. Behind it was a small room and a heavy steel door which had a mailbox-like setup with glass tubing poking out. Jerome pulled out a small plastic tube and poured its contents in. Apparently, there was a limited set of DNA sequences for each night the Spliceasy was open, which got circulated in advance. In the marketplaces, an up-to-date one went for a token equivalent of a couple of thousand dollars.

The door buzzed and swung slowly open, revealing spiral stairs. We descended into a low-lit space. The walls had art deco accents and living bioluminescent ferns. The centrepiece was a massive bar with a backlit glass display of colorful liquids and weird preserved specimens I hoped were fake. A Luminary singer crooned a Zephyra Lux cover into a retro microphone on a small stage, their skin covered in scales that shimmered in the UV light.

At the bottom of the stairs, two large bouncers frisked us, took away our Eyes and my Aspis for safekeeping, although they let us keep our Senselets. The Spliceasy took privacy extremely seriously, and most patrons were masked with face recognition spoofing LEDs. I drank the surroundings in. I'd lived in my own tiny corner of Darkome, but Darkome contained multitudes, including this crowd: high-end bio-hackers who had tech or biotech day jobs, and the Darkome equivalent of Burning Man's sparkleponies – the tourists who checked out the scene for the cool and the edge, but didn't really understand the underlying values. The crowd looked like a glow-in-the-dark alien parasite had attacked a flapper party. It was a bit pretentious but at the same time fantastic. I felt strangely euphoric.

I tugged at Jerome's sleeve. 'Come on. Let's get a drink.'

He frowned. 'We don't want to be late.'

'We're early,' I shouted over the crowd. 'I perform better with a slight buzz. And I can always do a FGF21 demo if needed. Let's go!'

Jerome grinned and elbow-ploughed a way for us to the bar. In a few minutes, we were holding a Synthetica (me) and a Neural Network (Jerome) in glass beakers. My drink's base was some kind of clear liquor with a splash of fluorescent blue curaçao, garnished with a small vial of extra liquid in a silver chain. Jerome's was darker, maybe rum or whisky based, with a web of golden tendrils on the surface. We toasted. Jerome drank half of his in one go, and put the rest on the counter. Synthetica tasted of vodka and fruit juices and warmed my belly, but some of his tension had rubbed off on me. Maybe he was right: I was taking this too lightly. I put my drink down without finishing it and nodded.

'Let's go see the big cheese,' I shouted in his ear over the noise.

He steered us through the bio-flappers, molls and mad scientists to a narrow corridor with what looked like private rooms. A man and a woman stood outside one of them, both compact and muscular, with short-shorn hair. They seemed to recognise Jerome and opened the door for us.

We entered a small room with dark wood panels, a cabinet of more preserved creature features and a round poker table. A man was sitting there, wearing Eyes – whoever he was, he had the clout to violate the privacy protocols. A fedora on the table was his only concession to the Spliceasy dress code.

He looked like he was in his early forties, with an angular, deeply tanned face. His combed-back blond-grey hair had a widow's peak, and the tight black T-shirt showed off a toned physique. If I was Kato, I thought, this guy was Doc Savage.

When he saw us, he took off his Eyes. He grinned at Jerome and looked at me curiously. His gaze felt like a lidar that scanned in every point and stored a full 3D model of me behind that high forehead. He stood up and gave Jerome a quick tight hug.

'Mr Brown!' His warm voice made my palms tickle oddly. 'And this must be your anonymous friend.' He loomed over me and took my hand in a practised grip. He smelled of a sporty aftershave. 'And how would you prefer to be called tonight, miss?' he asked.

'Sereia. Nice to meet you.' Sereia2019 was my Darkome username, something that was already obvious from my role as the *aspis-offleash* project admin.

He smiled. His eyes seemed slightly unfocused, but I had never met anyone who felt so fully *there*, almost more real than the room we were in.

'It is *such* a pleasure to meet you, Sereia,' he said. 'You can call me DzoGene.'

My heart beat faster. Linking his Darkome identity to his real face and not wearing a mask like Jerome and I did was a bit of a flex, showing that he didn't have anything to fear from someone like me. Also: *DzoGene*. I recognised the voice from the vircasts. In real life, his Slavic accent was stronger, similar to Svetlana's. The Siberian fox avatar's body language was there, too – that curious forward-leaning posture.

Jerome saw understanding dawning on my face and winked. Even retired, DzoGene had enough followers to turn *aspis-offleash* into an overnight success with a single post or a token donation.

'Hi,' I said, not wanting to appear starstruck. 'I used to watch your shows.'

'Ah! I'm glad you enjoyed them! I'm afraid I've had to focus on other things than creative projects recently. Young Jerome here has been most helpful on that front, so when he said there was someone I *had* to meet, I of course took it very seriously. Love the outfit, by the way. I thought the speakeasy setting was thematically appropriate, with the Z-L Act looming.'

'What do you think is going to happen?' I asked.

'Oh, it's going to pass, no doubt about it. They are still working through amendments, but it's going to go to floor debate and vote in a couple of weeks.' His tone was cheery, and I frowned.

'And you are not worried about that?'

He pressed his palms together, fingertips at his lips, and leaned forward. 'I'm not. Because it's good for Darkome. It's like the Prohibition. Right now, we are weirdos. After Z-L, we'll be gangsters and heroes. In my opinion, the community has become timid and stale. Zephyra, bless her, was on the cutting edge, and the most daring thing she did was enhanced empathy? Come on. We can do better than that.'

'What about the communities?' I asked, anger creeping into my voice. 'What about places like the Harbour? They might have to dissolve and go underground.'

'You are absolutely right.' DzoGene grew serious instantly. 'That would be an enormous loss. My own primary residence is in a Darkome community, and Jerome has told me much about the Harbour. You only have to go to The Labrynth on the Esplanade every Burning Man to see what they can do.'

I raised my eyebrows. The Labrynth was the Harbour camp at the Burning Man. The centrepiece was an actual labyrinth that the community reinvented and changed every year. One of my biggest bucket list items was to help build it one day.

'Sounds like you are a Burner,' I said. 'What if the Burn goes with the Z-L Act as well?'

'Don't despair, Captain. In my experience, this kind of legislation often gets enforced very selectively. The Bay Area has always been more accepting than the rest of the country. There are loopholes in any system of rules, by definition. Gödel's Theorem, you know.'

I *did* know, not least because it had been a DzoGene schtick in one of his casts where he interviewed ManchesterBabyo about incorporating DNA computing into the base Darkome stack, but I said nothing. Was he hinting at some kind of political influence that could protect the Harbour from what was coming? Was that what Jerome had secretly been working on? Suddenly, I regretted being so harsh on him.

DzoGene pursed his lips. 'And I suppose that is as good a segue as any into tonight's topic,' he said. 'Jerome tells me you have discovered an interesting loophole yourself. I had a chance to review the project. An enjoyable little demo. A stealth sequence to get things past an Aspis? As they say, big if true.'

Jerome leaned forward. 'It absolutely is,' he said. 'We have—'

DzoGene held up a hand. 'Let's hear it from Sereia herself.'

'It's true,' I said. 'Want to try it?' I held up my remaining vial of stealth-sequenced FGF21 mRNA and my electroporator.

'Thank you, but I don't drink. It wouldn't be hard to find volunteers, especially in this place – but of course, your exploit is going to be useless fairly soon, now that you've published it. Oh, it will take some time, given it has attracted so little attention to date. But Aspis *will* update their firmware to counteract it, sooner or later. Mikko Repo, Aspis's chief security officer, is no fool, and has more respect for Darkome than his boss.'

That took me off guard. So far, I had felt almost like a guest in a DzoGene cast episode, a sounding board for his rants and opinions until he got me to open up and tell my story. But this was no safe interview space. My stomach fell. I felt like an idiot for not having even thought about Aspis scouring Darkome for jailbreaking attempts. Creating a Darkome account was not trivial, it involved a real-life multi-party DNA key exchange – but of course a company like Aspis had the resources to get in if they needed to. And it was always possible that a Darkome user would sell the zero-day to Aspis for a bounty.

I took a deep breath. 'Well, that is exactly why we are looking for off-Darkome financing. To carry on our work off-line until we are ready. That sequence was just an example. I have an engine that can generate more Aspis zero-days.' More specifically, I *wished* that was the case. The Heffalump pulsed under my skin. I was sure the basic maths held up, but biology was complicated, and Aspis did have a *lot* of computers. I pulled out a small square card, a dot of DNA-stored data in the middle, and slid it across the table. 'See for yourself.'

The DNA repo on the card contained several other stealth sequences I had managed to mine from my Aspis data in the last couple of days, some homologous to the first one I'd found, some completely different. I knew that the Aspis did not detect them, but had not tested them with any synthetic mRNA constructs – which of course might interfere with their function. But *some* of them would probably work. The Heffalump was not a one-trick pachyderm. Surely DzoGene would see that.

With practised hands, he fed the card to a darkreader,

a card case-sized open hardware nanopore sequencer designed for reading Darkome sneakernet data. I looked at it with some jealousy: they were beyond my limited token means and in his situation, I would be doing sample prep and feeding my MinION for a couple of hours. But I was grateful that it only took seconds to transfer the data to his Eyes, otherwise the tension would have been unbearable.

Spiderwebs of data flashed in DzoGene's Eyes with blazing speed. Jerome reached over and touched my shoulder. The minutes seemed to stretch into hours.

Finally, DzoGene leaned back in his chair. His eyes glinted appreciatively. 'Well, Sereia, you certainly know how to make things interesting. I'm *dying* to know how you are generating these. In silico?' He drummed on the table with the fingertips of both hands. 'Don't tell me. You are actually modelling the DNA-nanopore complex of the sequencer at a quantum level.' He pointed a finger at me. 'The only way that's possible is if you have access to Enigma's new entangled neural field model. The hundred billion dollar one.'

He looked at Jerome and clapped him on the shoulder. 'You sly fox. Did you actually get in already without telling me?'

I kept my face impassive, but I had no idea what he was talking about. Jerome looked uncomfortable and shook his head. 'We're still working on that,' he said hastily. 'This is something else.' I could see sweat beading on his upper lip. Seeing him with DzoGene made it obvious where a lot of his mannerisms came from. He was trying to mirror his idol – who also scared the shit out of him. That sent a little shiver down my spine. What was I getting myself into?

DzoGene looked disappointed. Then his grin flashed back

on. 'Curiouser and curiouser,' he said. 'I'm begging for a breadcrumb here, Sereia.' His eyes were so puppy-like and pleading that I couldn't stop myself laughing.

'Breadcrumbs will cost you,' I said.

He laughed, showing white canines. 'Fair enough, fair enough! All right. Let's say I believe you have a miracle machine, or an oracle, or a genie. If I help you, what are you going to do with it?'

I leaned back, crossing my arms, hands disappearing into the oversized sleeves.

'What would *you* do with it?' I asked.

'Ha! That is exactly the right question.' He held my gaze with his own. The intensity was almost dizzying.

'Allow me, then, to lay out a trail of breadcrumbs of my own. Please indulge me by following it. Since you are familiar with my work, you are aware that I've had a long-standing interest in improving the human condition. The reason I stopped the casts was that I became acutely concerned about the approaching inevitability of human extinction.'

15

Gingerbread

DzoGene spread his hands. 'I know, I know. It's not fashionable to talk about AI risk, these days, humanity's destruction at the hands of an artificial superintellect. You are too young to remember the mortal terror we lived with in the 2020s. I, on the other hand, am old enough to remember the fear of nuclear war, and this was worse.'

I raised my eyebrows. DzoGene had to be a *lot* older than he looked.

'We were barrelling off a cliff, with no one in charge,' he continued. 'At that time, I had already had some success in business, and made investments in AI safety research, as did other philanthropists. But we were too few and too late.

'But the transformer scaling laws plateaued in the late twenties and then the Decade of Plagues gave us both a hardware AI winter with the breaking of semiconductor supply chains, and a real basis for strict regulation of AI personas and agents. For all practical purposes, the AI safety prophets won. I thought we had dodged a bullet, and focused on the beautiful explosion in biology that we are both so familiar with. I even finally agreed to have children with my wife.'

DzoGene flattened his Eyes into handheld touchscreen mode and held up a photo of a little dark-haired girl with a gap-toothed grin. 'This is my daughter. She is now three years old.

'But now the ground is rumbling beneath our feet again. I first felt the tremors with the Kimura and Lin paper. Quantum Entangled Neural Fields or QENFs, true distributed non-local machine learning with a genuine quantum advantage and scaling laws that were logarithmic, not exponential. A paradigm shift. But they required expensive quantum hardware, and were – in the absence of quantum datasets – even more data hungry than the classical models. So I handwaved my concerns away. We would have time to get ready, this time, I thought. My daughter would have time to grow up.

'And then Alex Omondi came along.'

DzoGene sighed. 'I should highlight that I bear him no personal malice. I've met him briefly, and he is a lovely, gentle, warm human. Like a little boy, a Christopher Robin with his AIs, you know. Enthusiastic. Utterly committed to Christian values. Wants the best for everyone. But he is quite possibly going to kill us all.

'He figured out how to put together the compute and datasets to train QENFs. The key innovation was financial. There is a way to fund large climate projects—'

'Climate-Adjusted Value Creation Instrument,' I interjected. It was how the Mojave Bloom Project Dad worked for was funded.

'Very good, Captain,' DzoGene said. 'That's precisely it. Omondi went to all the big climate infrastructure funds and told them what a giant QENF could do – solar panel design, fusion reactor control systems, climate modelling. All that potential was packaged into securities that he used to raise the billions he needed. Using those resources, Enigma has now finished training a new model called Nyoka. Jerome, maybe you can tell us about Nyoka.'

Jerome leaned forward, less nervous now. 'Enigma is going to announce Nyoka in a few weeks and give beta access to select partners. The name comes from the Swahili word for snake. From what we have been able to piece together, the total amount of capital Enigma amassed for training Nyoka was in excess of a hundred billion dollars. They have built a network of quantum computing facilities all over the world, with their own fusion reactors.'

'So what?' I asked. 'Sounds like we are going to get better solar panels, better AI assistants. That's a good thing, surely?'

Jerome's expression was grim. 'Omondi got a new tattoo. A snake eating its own tail. I have a source claiming that Nyoka can do recursive self-improvement. Quantum search through possible architectures. And Enigma's safety team is now working overtime. Another rumour is that Nyoka has been starting to display agent-like behaviour, actually trying to implement the improvements.'

'How do you know all this?' I asked, although I could make some guesses. Mallory and Jerome had got into Enigma Labs two years ago and stolen one of their old models. It sounded like Jerome had made his way even deeper into the company since then.

'We can set that aside for now,' DzoGene said. 'The important thing is that we have at least medium confidence in Mr Brown's intel.' He looked anxious, cradling his flattened

Eyes in his hands. 'My daughter lost her first baby tooth yesterday,' he said. 'My wife and I are now worried that she won't see her tenth birthday. Not unless we somehow keep up.'

Fuck, I thought. Maybe I had completely missed the fact that the world was about to end. It was obvious that Jerome believed it too. But there were still pieces missing.

'OK, so assuming this is not just a rumour, this thing can improve itself. How is that bad? You said Enigma has AI safety people. Omondi sounds smart. How does this translate to everyone dying?'

DzoGene looked grim. 'Rapidly evolving systems can't be caged. If Nyoka can change itself, it is able to change any goal we set for it. It's an old AI safety research result that in that scenario, it converges on instrumental goals. Obtaining resources. Eliminating anything in its way. We may simply not be smart enough for evolution-robust AI alignment.'

I wasn't entirely convinced, but the point about evolving systems and cages hit home. The Heffalump was living proof of biology finding a way. But I had sat in on conversations like this before, at the Dark Star BBQ in the Harbour – AI alignment, the Simulation Argument. I thought of Mallory, who was always quick to pounce on anyone who didn't act according to their purported beliefs.

'So ... if you really buy all this,' I said, 'why aren't you trying to get smarter? Upgrading yourself right now? Or others? Maybe all it takes is a smarter DzoGene or Yudkowsky or Omondi to figure out the AI safety part. Why aren't you putting your money where your mouth is?'

DzoGene pointed a finger at Jerome. 'You didn't tell me she was so sharp! Very good!' He turned back to me. 'Two reasons. First, with radical enhancements – whether for cognition or brain-computer interfaces – it is very easy to get things wrong. Trust me, I know.'

He took a small case from his pocket, opened it, bent his head back and removed what looked like silvery contact lenses from his eyes. He placed them in the case very carefully and blinked a few times. His eyes were amber now, completely unfocused and blank. 'I funded a team in the late twenties to build a brain-computer interface prototype. They used an AAV vector to deliver an optogenetic payload to my visual cortex. My brain's immune cells didn't like that. I nearly died from something like viral meningitis. There is a dark hole in the back of my head.'

He held up the case. 'Fortunately, the brain is plastic. It can learn to use any input. These lenses send video to an implant in my auditory cortex. I spent a long time in the dark, in a vast roar of noise, but then the brain region that processed sound rewired itself to see. The world looks different now, but at least there is light. So when it comes to human enhancement, I am actually more safety-conscious than you might think, Sereia.'

I stared into his unseeing eyes, the old guilt-snake squirming in my belly.

'I get that. My ... my mom died because of ... a mistake,' I said. 'An mRNA synthesis error.'

DzoGene nodded. 'I appreciate you sharing that. As you know, the Aspis and the other mRNA chips have optimised microfluidic synthesis, error correction and quality control. If only we could tell them to make what we wanted.'

He put his prostheses back on, squinting and blinking until his intense gaze was back. 'But that's not all. Whatever means we use to level humanity up, is it really worth it if we can't do it for *everyone*? Or – all sentient beings? Dogs, cats, dolphins, apes, octopi? Otherwise, we are perpetuating intelligence inequality. We of Darkome forget that we are privileged. We have skills, knowledge, that only few possess. But almost everyone has an Aspis.

'Can you glimpse the shape of the gingerbread house now, Sereia? Can you see why I am interested in your project?'

I could see it. Open, jailbroken Aspises for all, programmable with a thought. A way to deploy all the latent ideas languishing in Darkome projects, all at once. Everyone able to share the most advanced cognitive upgrade. And since *you* controlled your Aspis, the power to choose your biology. Your future.

Outside, the Luminary singer began another song, something French and sad, Nina Simone.

Something about this didn't feel quite right. I had the same uncomfortable feeling when Jerome made me listen to DzoGene's casts. There had always been something I fundamentally disagreed with him on, even if his eloquence and verbosity made it difficult to pin down.

I remembered Svetlana's words. *Lots of people will want it.* I thought I recognised the look in DzoGene's prosthetic eyes: like Amanda Shah, during the hearing. Telling a story he believed in, but leaving something essential out. And trying to make me feel like I was the most important person in the world.

I looked at Jerome. He drank in DzoGene's every word.

'I'll be honest with you,' DzoGene said. 'I had already decided to back your project before this meeting. I simply needed to be sure our values and vision were aligned. I will provide all the resources you need, within reason, cash, crypto, lab space, all that can be arranged.

'Not only that, I would love to be your thought partner in this, and work closely with you to map out how we maximise the impact. Jerome will co-ordinate and set up a DAO with a simple decision-making structure. Congratulations.'

He got up and held out his hand.

There it was. Once again, someone else wanted to control my future.

I stood up as well, looking at his hand, hesitating.

'That is ... incredibly generous,' I said slowly. 'I can't tell you how much I appreciate your faith in our project. But this has been a lot to take in. I will need to think about it, if that's all right with you.'

DzoGene pulled his hand back and studied me carefully. 'Of course. But time grows short.' He stroked his chin. 'Are you positive I can't convince you, right here and now? Name your terms, and I'm sure we can make something work.'

Suddenly, I wanted to talk to Holst and Mallory really badly. This was getting far too big and complicated. Svetlana had been right. It had been a mistake to go to Jerome first.

'Sorry,' I said. 'There are some other ... stakeholders I need to consult.' Jerome's eyes went wide with shock, all piratical swagger gone.

'I understand,' DzoGene said softly. 'Well, in that case, surely you won't begrudge me making a small token donation to your existing Darkome project, to show that I am serious? To put my money where my mouth is, so to speak?'

He unfolded his Eyes and put them back on. 'There.'

My darksense buzzed in a pattern that I had rarely experienced. A *significant* amount of tokens had landed in the project tip jar. Then it buzzed again. And again. Given the quadratic voting system on Darkome, where token donations required exponentially more tokens as the scale increased, DzoGene was really splurging.

'Thank you, but token-based support for this project stub was not what we were asking for—'

I almost bit my tongue when I saw the trap around me snapping shut.

There was no way to refuse a token donation to an existing project, and the donor usernames were public. DzoGene's followers would be checking out the project and making their own donations. It would spread like wildfire. Soon, people would be experimenting with the stealth sequence, starting their own projects, attracting a snowball of attention.

Including from Aspis.

I unclenched my teeth. 'What the hell are you doing?'

'Sereia dear, I am a humble Darkome user who believes in your project. I can't help but support it. I'm sure you understand.'

More darksense buzzes. It all clicked together in my head.

'Aspis ... Aspis is going to be all over this now,' I whispered. The minute another stealth sequence application popped up, they would close the first loophole. Given what Shah had publicly said, they couldn't afford to lose face over a security vulnerability. They would come after the project, hard. Sock puppet accounts on Darkome to pose as collaborators and sow discord. Cyber-attacks on Darkome hardware. And that was before they found out who was behind the original exploit.

Before they found me.

My hands started shaking violently, and I hid them inside the long sleeves.

'You can't have rebel heroes without the Empire, Captain,' DzoGene said. 'Trust me. An enemy will help you focus on what matters, and who your friends are. My offer stands. If you want my help, you only have to ask.'

'This isn't what we talked about,' Jerome said. 'This isn't—'

'Mr Brown.' DzoGene's voice was like a whip. 'I trust you will help Sereia arrive at the right decision in the next twenty-four hours. In the meantime, I believe you are overdue a report on your other project. It would be a shame if this one became too much of a distraction and we were forced to reconsider our arrangement. Do I make myself clear?'

Jerome swallowed hard and nodded.

I looked back at DzoGene, trying to keep my composure. 'Thank you, DzoGene. We'll keep you informed about our progress, and any decisions.'

'I look forward to it,' he said with a radiant grin. 'Good luck.'

I went back to the noise of the Spliceasy. Jerome hesitated, looked back at the private room's door, but then followed. In a few moments, we had our Eyes back and emerged outside in the damp evening air.

I walked down the dirty alley with long strides, feeling nauseous. Jerome ran after me.

'Inara, wait! I swear I didn't know he was going to do that! That's not who he is, trust me. This is to make you realise what's really important. He's a visionary. We should go back and talk it over—'

I stopped and whipped round. 'Does he know my real name? My real identity?'

'No! Of course not!'

'But he knows yours, you idiot. It's not hard to draw a line from you to me. If he wants to, he can leak my name to Aspis any time. Unless I dance to whatever insane tune is playing inside that head of his. What the hell were you thinking, Jerome? What does this guy have on you?'

'He ... it doesn't matter. I got into some trouble after you left, and he helped me out of it, OK? I owe him. But it's more than that. You heard what he said. The Nyoka risk is real. I don't think your Heffalump is an accident, Inara. It's ... I don't know, do you remember what Holst said about the mycelium, links across space and time? Sometimes we are given gifts when we need them the most. Would you please reconsider? You said you would trust me, that we'd be partners. Well, I found someone who can help us. Don't throw this away. Please.'

'Who is he, really? Who is DzoGene?'

He swallowed. 'He ... his real name is Dimitry Soloviov. He's been involved with Darkome from the start, but that's not all he does. He invests in Darkome-spun projects and actual companies, too. He lives in Xanadu, a Darkome community in Cuba, usually, but you never know where he's going to turn up.

'I'm so sorry, Inara. I would never have brought you here if I had known he'd threaten you like this. You have to believe me. But Dimitry sees the big picture like no one else. He can get to anyone. It's almost supernatural. And he has a plan—'

'Stop,' I said.

I looked at Jerome and suddenly I saw the helpless little boy in a burning house he really was underneath, waiting for someone to save him. And now he had lit my world on fire as well. My thoughts ran higgledy-piggledy in all directions, looking for a way out. I had to find a quiet place to think.

But at least one thing was now clear.

'You were right the first time, Jerome. This really was a mistake. A big one.'

'You don't understand. He's not bluffing, Inara. He's going to follow through with this if you don't co-operate. I won't be able to protect you unless you work with me. With him.'

I took off my fedora and goggles and ran my fingers along my scalp. I only needed to say yes to get everything I wanted. Or was that really true? Everything DzoGene – Soloviov – had said had made me feel like the most important person in the world. But there had been something alien lurking beneath his tanned skin, like one of Svetlana's *zmeyove*, a shape-shifting dragon in human form. He had been ready to sacrifice the Harbour to radicalise Darkome. You could justify almost anything to save humanity from an existential threat. And Jerome was completely under the spell.

I had to show him that dragons could be beaten.

I let out a breath I had been holding in.

'I'm not going to do that, Jerome,' I said quietly. 'Not with someone who wants to put me on a leash like that. Not ever.'

He looked at me. 'You're crazy. Aspis *will* come after you. You'll have to run.'

'You ... you could run with me,' I said. 'Whatever he has

over you, we can figure it out. Together. Just the two of us, like before.'

Jerome's face, pale and perfect in the streetlights, was full of pain.

'I can't, Inara,' he whispered. 'I really can't.'

'OK,' I said in a small voice, tears in my eyes. 'I see. I . . . I hope you find what you are looking for, Jerome.'

He took the metallic flower from his lapel and pressed it into my hand. I held it limply.

'I'll make sure you'll have twenty-four hours. I can do that at least. I'll tell Dimitry I'm trying to convince you. I'll buy you more time, if I can.' He put on his Eyes and flicked me a crypto transfer with a finger, ten thousand dollars' worth. 'That's all I have. You can't go to the Harbour, even if—' *Even if Mallory and Holst make an exception to their sacred rule*, I completed the thought. 'Anyway, Aspis would know to look for you there. Get out of the country. Mexico, maybe. Or – don't tell me. Better I don't know.'

'Thank you,' I said. 'And – you can stop now. I'll figure it out. You've – you've helped enough.'

He took a few backwards steps, arms at his sides, a shadow on his cheek like his old scar. Then he turned and started jogging down the street, dress shoes ringing on the pavement. I started after him for a minute, then turned around, and broke into a run.

16

Hidden Hearts

I ran all the way back to Dolores Heights, slowing down only on the steep slope on 21st Street that led up to the Haunted House. The wind chilled the sweat on my skin. The darksense on my wrist buzzed to the rhythm of my frantic heartbeat. *aspis-offleash* was going viral on Darkome. Every token that came in was another brick in the jail that Soloviov was building around me, and I couldn't see a way out.

At the top of the hill, an expansive view of San Francisco opened up. The Salesforce Tower gleamed neon pink. A rising mist blurred the city lights into a soft golden halo. The Aspis Spire loomed to the east, a silver-and-glass spiral, more like something designed by elves than the Dark Tower it was. I imagined a blazing eye at its apex, searching for me, and shivered.

Twenty-four hours, I thought. How far can I get in twenty-four hours?

The Haunted House was quiet when I entered. The lights were on in the kitchen and a powerful smell of overcooked tomatoes drifted into the hallway. I was starving, but could not face Thanh in my present state. At least I now had enough crypto to cover the late payments. I set a timer for the transaction to go through the next day so Thanh wouldn't come to check up on me, included a month's extra, and stepped quietly up the stairs. Svetlana's room was dark: she had to be out, working.

In my room, I peeled off the sweat-soiled gangster outfit and paced around in my bathrobe. A spring coiled ever tighter in my empty stomach. The darksense buzzed joyously, so I put on my Eyes and checked the *aspis-offleash* project page. Over a thousand donated tokens and going up. Linked projects were already popping into being.

mRNA delivery of fibroelastic proteins into vocal cords for supernatural singing voice.

Switching off sense of taste to support dieting.

Growing pearls under your skin with injected mollusc protein mRNA.

LuxLives, a project to duplicate Zephyra's mirror neuron activating payload, but incorporating the stealth sequence – on impulse, I bookmarked that one.

It was exactly what I had wanted.

Disgusted, I closed the Darkome app and flopped down on my beanbag, staring at the ceiling. I should have been running, I knew, but I had nowhere to go. I played it out in my head: Aspis lawsuit, getting kicked out of PROSPERITY-A, probably jailtime. Unemployment. Living on universal basic somewhere in the module communities in the Midwest. Getting cancer, over and over.

No. I could not live like that. There had to be a better way.

I picked up Mom's notebooks, ran my fingers over her

handwriting, smelled the yellowed pages. What would she have done?

Suddenly, I remembered our evening prayers. Mom was a lapsed Catholic, but she had kept that as our evening ritual, before sleep. And she always prayed before anything important. Just in case, she said.

I folded my hands and closed my eyes. If there was a God, I wanted them to be like Holst's mycelium: connections across space and time. *Sometimes we are given gifts when we need them the most*, Jerome had said. *Hey, you out there*, I thought. *I need something. Anything.*

I don't know how long I sat like that. I might have fallen asleep. Then my Eyes pinged and startled me to alertness. I picked them up in flatscreen mode and saw a message from Svetlana.

> Hey! How did your meeting go? Still at work, but thought I'd check in.

> Long story, I typed. > Jerome's contact turned out to be a zmey. It didn't go well.

> Shit. That's not good.

> How do you destroy them? I asked.

The three dots blinked for a time. Then Svetlana's response popped up.

> You find their hidden heart and destroy it. Or you can show them their true face in a mirror, and they kill themselves. We'll talk about it when I get home, OK?

A warm feeling bloomed in my chest.

> OK. Love you. You're a good friend.

The L-word slipped out. I hadn't used it for two years. It felt good.

> Hey. I'm living vicariously through you, sestrentse. Cheers! Stay safe.

If I ran, there would be no time to say goodbye to Svetlana, but I couldn't bring myself to do it via text. I shook myself. I was being a coward again, not a dragonslayer. I turned Svetlana's words around in my mind. Fairy tales always had a seed of truth in them. *True face in a mirror.* What did that mean in this case? I had no idea. *Hidden heart* made more sense, classic high fantasy plot, destroy the magic thing that gives the bad guy their power—

The image of the Aspis Spire towering over the city flashed before my eyes. I *had* items of power: the new zero-day stealth sequences I had not yet published.

Companies bought zero-days from hackers, with cash, and with … immunity from prosecution. If Jerome's promise was any good, I still had twenty-four hours. I could simply walk into Mordor and make a deal with Sauron.

I sat bolt upright. That was it. Soloviov had even told me who I needed to speak to. Go to Mikko Repo, trade the sequences I had for protection. Maybe even access to Panacea Store. A part of me recoiled at the thought. But the alternative was running – and my connection to the Harbour would draw Aspis's attention to it even before the Z-L Act passed, before Holst, Mallory and the others were ready. They might hate me, Darkome might hate me, but I could buy them time – and I would have a shot at something resembling freedom.

'OK,' I whispered to myself. 'Yeah. Let's do this.'

Suddenly, I was completely awake and alert. I grabbed a towel and ran downstairs into the shower, not caring about the noise. I didn't even wait for the water to warm up, and the cold shock felt good. I washed hastily, using the chilly downpour as a forcing function to be quick. I brushed the Heffalump by accident. It was noticeably bigger, which wasn't good – but if things went according to plan, I wouldn't need it any more. I ignored the crawling whispersense and turned the water off.

Back in my room, I put on my regular clothes – jeans, Mom's Captain America T-shirt for luck, cycling jacket, cap. Then I packed essentials. I couldn't be sure I would be coming back. Into the backpack went the MinION, the multichannel pipette, some basic reagents, Mom's notebooks, clothes, toiletries, Peixinho. I picked up Jerome's seahorse and flower, sighed and threw them in, too.

I had tokens to burn, so I set a few wheels in motion. I dictated a quick summary of the recent events to Donnie and had the AI turn it into a complete narrative. I sent it to Holst and Mallory via PigeonPost, a Darkome service that encoded encrypted text into DNA and sent it securely to a given user through the dead drop network. I couldn't leave them completely in the dark and wanted them to understand why I was doing what I was about to do. I took an empty page from one of Mom's notebooks and wrote a quick farewell note to Svetlana by hand.

Then it was time to go.

I took one last look around the room and turned off the lights, leaving my life for the past two years behind. I headed downstairs, slipped the note under Svetlana's door, and called a self-drive to Aspis's campus in Mission Bay.

While I waited for the car, I stood outside and looked at the house that had been my first grown-up home, and thought about all my housemates who had passed through it. I wished I had got to know them better. Maybe they had secrets and kindness inside them like Svetlana.

Or maybe they were dangerous to get close to, like me.

The lights of my approaching car killed my night vision, and the blue outline of the House faded into the dark. I got in and breathed in the new car smell of the high-end Tesla I had booked for the ride. If I was riding to my doom, I might as well do it in style.

I leaned back and started going through my plan while doing boxed breathing. Four in, hold four, four out, hold four. Four in, hold four, four out, hold four.

It was going to be a long night.

Part Three

The Spire, 2041

17

The Dance of Life

The sprawling Aspis campus was generally open to the public, except for the buildings themselves. When I entered, my Eyes immediately offered me an AR tour, which I declined.

The campus had eaten most of what had been the Mission Bay biotech hub around University of California's San Francisco campus. The Spire was the centrepiece, of course, but there were other buildings in organic shapes, like the main R&D hub, a circular structure with a honeycomb facade. There were winding walkways through green areas, small cafés and sculpture gardens. It smelled of freshly cut grass. It was past nine in the evening, but the lights were on in many of the buildings, and I passed small groups of Aspis employees talking loudly. The scale of it made me feel like a virus entering the body of a host, vast organs looming around me, while I prayed to go unnoticed by the immune system.

Up close, the Spire was breathtaking: two entwining columns, with horizontal passages in between, in four different hues of glass, twisting upwards until it seemed to pierce the overcast sky. Of course, there was a security check-in you needed to go through to access the lobby, but I had taken that into account.

This was my least favourite part of the plan. I fidgeted with the strap of my backpack while waiting for the right moment as I walked along a path leading to the Spire. A group of three staffers approached, and I got ready to make my move. My mouth was suddenly dry. *I'm terrible at this,* I thought. *They'll see through me and call security. I'll never get in.*

But I had to try.

The group approached, talking loudly like it was the most natural thing conceivable to be in the heart of the most powerful biotech company in the world, one which held the remote control for almost everyone's immune system. There was a kind-faced man in a blue Aspis hoodie, a woman with black hair in a ponytail and round glasses, and a serious blond man with a neatly trimmed beard. They belonged here. I thought about the route that they had taken – Ivy League schools, maybe Stanford compsci dropouts. Things I could never do.

'Uh, hey,' I said, and seized up, unable to get the words out. The bearded man frowned, and I forced myself to continue. 'Sorry. Do you work here?'

They looked at me for a second, and then the man in the hoodie gave me half a smile.

'Yeah, we do. What about you?'

I was doing this all wrong, thinking of them as corporate drones. These people were proud of what they did here. I thought about Dad and how everyone he met instinctively liked him. He'd once said you had to assume they were good and trustworthy, and more often than not, that made them so.

'Haha, no, maybe one day!' I said, trying to bring that feeling into my voice. 'I'm studying art at NYU, and ... well, this is really stupid. I'm in town for the day. My lecturer told me to check out *The Dance of Life* in the Spire lobby and make a sketch.' The words came easily now. 'The day ran away with me, and now I can't get in any more. I was wondering if any of you could help me to take a quick look? I need like, five minutes.'

The woman, who seemed to be the highest ranking member of the group, gave me a curious look. I smiled at her shyly.

'Yeah, you shouldn't really miss it if you are here,' she said. 'I don't see why not. We're going to pass through there in a second, so tag along. But make sure you stay with us. I can sign you in as a limited access guest. Don't try to leave the lobby, though, or you'll get into trouble with security.'

'Thank you so much! Do you guys always work so late?'

'Nah,' the bearded man said. 'There's a bit of a fire drill going on. Usually it's more relaxed. But our misfortune is your fortune. Come along, it's this way.'

'You guys are stars. I'll be out of your hair in no time, I promise.'

The group took me through the checkpoint and into the dizzyingly high lobby. I stared at the huge kinetic sculpture hanging overhead. It was made from hundreds of shimmering ribbons that moved with air currents, changing colour constantly, swaying and intertwining. I had planned to make a show of gawking at it, but for a moment I was captivated. I knew from the brief research I'd done that the ribbons were covered in living biofilms. As they brushed against each other, the bacteria in them exchanged genes, passing around biological circuits that made the patterns evolve and change.

This is what the future should be like, I thought. An endless dance of becoming.

The woman in the blazer touched my shoulder. 'It's quite something, isn't it? We had the artist, Aria Vega, give a talk once. It took her five years to put it together.'

'Wow,' I said. 'It's ... thank you. I'm glad I got to see it.'

'Don't mention it,' she said. 'Good luck with your project.' She waved a hand and caught up with the rest of her group. They got into a blob-shaped elevator that climbed up one of the interior columns rapidly.

I felt naked and alone standing in the middle of the vast space, and shook myself. So Amanda Shah had good taste in art. That didn't change what I needed to do.

I put on my Eyes and approached the circular desk in the centre of the lobby. It was staffed by a depressingly alert-looking human: late twenties, auburn hair in a loose bun, strands framing a round face. Her hazel eyes were alight with the same enthusiasm the group who I'd entered with had radiated. Her name tag said *Heather*.

'Hi!' she said perkily. 'How can I help you?'

'I'm here to see Mikko Repo,' I said. Her gaze flickered as she consulted her Eyes. She pursed her lips. 'I'm so sorry. It's very late, and it doesn't look like you have an appointment.'

'I will, once he sees this.' I tossed her a file that contained one of the new jailbreak sequences. 'Tell him or his team to run that through their nanopore-DNA complex models. They'll want to see it, trust me.'

Heather's eyes widened. 'I'm not sure I can —'

'Try it,' I said, using the same sharp tone that usually worked on Clementine and my other canine clients. 'Pretty sure he's around. After all, you have a zero-day crisis going on.'

'Can I at least have a name, or—'

I leaned forward, both hands on the counter. 'Sereia2019 will do. Make sure you tell him that, actually.'

Dumbfounded, she nodded. I spotted a fern garden on the other side of the lobby, next to an artificial waterfall. It seemed to hide a snack bar of some sort. Suddenly, I realised how hungry I was.

'I'm going to be over there, OK?' I told Heather. 'And tell him I don't have all night. There's more where that sequence came from, and there are ... other interested parties.'

Suddenly, Heather resembled a panicked rabbit. She typed furiously on a virtual keyboard and threw fearful looks at me between keystrokes. I hid behind the fern wall, sat down on a low bench and let out an explosive breath, glad she couldn't see my relieved expression. I was practically hyperventilating. Every breath felt like it was full of champagne bubbles, tickling and insubstantial.

Holy shit, I thought. This might actually work.

18

Partial Immunity

I grabbed a green juice and some kind of seaweed/vitrovegan shrimp wrap from the snack bar and hid among the ferns, munching on them. Elevated blood sugar put me on the edge again. I used one of the public restrooms and stared at my mirror image, rehearsing my lines in my head until they rang hollow. I returned to the benches by the waterfall and sat there, lost in the soft white noise, until a shadow fell over me.

He was huge and thick-bodied, with a lumbering gait. He had thinning brown hair offset by a luxurious beard, thick jutting eyebrows and a grumpy expression. He wore a many-pocketed leather jacket over an Aspis T-shirt.

'More where that came from, huh?' he said. He had a surprisingly boyish voice with a Nordic accent that made the consonants hard and flat.

I looked up but didn't stand, meeting his gaze. 'Yeah. Are you Mikko Repo?'

He leaned forward, hands on his knees, until his face was close to mine. His breath smelled of stale coffee.

'That's right,' he said. 'Although if you have something

to do with what's been happening tonight, you might want to call me Mr Repo, or better yet, Worst Nightmare.'

I held his gaze. He was really good at staring, but so was I: basic dog training dominance. His eyes were two angry pinpoints, and there was a spiderweb of fatigue lines around them.

'Nice to meet you, Worst,' I said. 'I'm Inara.'

'I know who you are. That's the part that doesn't make sense. What the hell is an ex-dogwalker with a Darkome username doing with a goddamn zero-day that ruined my Wednesday night?'

'Well, I gave it to you. Obviously.'

He straightened his back and poked my shoulder with a finger.

'Is this some kind of joke to you? We have people publishing dangerous shit on Darkome, and a whole bunch of idiots are dosing it. And it's not just the biohackers in their parents' basements who want to be the next Zephyra Lux. We caught an old Plague in New York, a Dreamweaver variant, spreading with your sequence. If they had released it a few hours earlier, we would have had a serious outbreak. Do you see me laughing, Miss Reyes?'

It was my turn to blink. My heart went cold. It made sense that in the same way that Aspis monitored Darkome, whoever the bad actors behind the Decade of Plagues were did too. And the impeding Z-L Act was going to push the more radical Darkome users to do extreme things. A yawning chasm opened up in my stomach when I thought about how stupid publishing the sequence in the first place had been.

'I ... didn't know about that,' I said quietly. 'I never meant that to happen.'

'Hmph. You lot never do. *Jeesus perkele*. It's a miracle we're still alive.' He rubbed his temples with stubby fingers. 'OK. You're here to sell me some more zero-days, right?'

'Yeah.'

'That's what I thought.' He turned and motioned me to follow. 'Come on. I need some more coffee if we're going to do this. And this had better not be any kind of social engineering scheme to get close to our hardware. I invented those.'

We got into one of the elevators. Two security guards trailed closely behind, stony-faced and muscular, with oddly bulging Aspis T-shirts and military grade Eyes. They kept a respectful distance from us.

When the elevator started moving, Repo edged away from the curving floor-to-ceiling window facing the lobby.

'I hate these bloody things,' he said.

'They're meant to be transcription factors, right? Binding to DNA.'

'Hah. So I'm told. A metal box would do for me, but I guess Aspis has a brand.'

'They should jump around, you know.'

'What?'

'If they are transcription factors. They have multiple binding sites. They should jump between them.'

Repo looked a little green. 'Fuck. That's a cheerful thought. Don't tell Shah that. She might get it into her head to make them more true to life.'

The elevator accelerated accompanied by a soft hum. We shot up one of the Spire's columns at blinding speed before coming to a sudden halt. Repo ushered us down a glass-walled corridor. I glimpsed meeting rooms, offices and VR pods, common areas full of whiteboards and bioart, and a giant aquarium wall of climate change-tolerant coral in spectacular colours. The Aspis logo was embedded in the living polyps.

We stopped at a small kitchenette looking out over the campus and Mission Bay. From the 40th floor, the Aspis campus around the Spire looked like a giant cell. The buildings were organelles, surrounded by the green cytoplasm of parks. I was right in the nucleus. It was all too much. My hands started shaking. I sat down on a chair near the window and folded my arms to hide my unease.

Mikko ignored me and set to work on a jet-engine-like chrome-plated espresso machine with expert hands and intense focus.

'Want some?' he asked once the machine started muttering. In spite of the adrenaline pounding in my veins, I nodded. It gave me a bit of time to study Repo. Appropriately for his position, he had a sparse online presence. He had sold a bio/cybersecurity firm to Aspis, co-founded with Tanya Khatri. He was forty-six. That was about it.

In a few moments, he gave me a small espresso cup that looked tiny in his bearlike hand. I accepted it gratefully.

He sipped his own with a pinky finger jutting out at an angle and sat down across from me with a thump.

'OK. Let's get to the bottom of this, before I go back to putting out the fires you lit.' He tapped his Eyes. 'I got three messages from Amanda while making espresso. We are pushing out a firmware update to three billion people to deal with your fun little surprise, so I need to keep this short. How many more exploits do you have and where the hell did they come from?'

I swallowed. 'I ... I need some assurances first.'

165

'Assurances? I'm telling you we nearly had a replay of the Decade of Plagues and you want assurances? You're young, kid, but you're old enough to go to jail. Tell me everything you know right now, and if it's real, maybe you won't. It's as simple as that.'

I sipped my own espresso. It was already a little cold but maybe the best I had ever tasted, bitter in exactly the right way.

'I have a hundred sequences,' I said slowly. 'I'll give them to you, unpublished, in exchange for two things. One: immunity from prosecution. Complete, no loopholes, no strings attached. I need to know I won't be thrown in jail for helping you. And two: I want Aspis support to develop a therapeutic for Li-Fraumeni Syndrome for Panacea Store. I'm talking about a real commitment: resources, expertise, the works.' I put the espresso cup down. 'Small price to pay to get your Wednesday nights back, don't you think?'

Repo looked at me, a surprised look on his face. 'Li-Fraumeni,' he muttered. 'Right. It was in your file.' He made a fist. 'Fucking biology. When it breaks, it really breaks, right? Look, kid. I can't offer you shit before I know if any of this holds up. Tell me where these sequences are coming from. Full method disclosure. After that, we can *maybe* talk assurances. Maybe. But not before.'

We stared at each other again.

'That,' I said finally, 'doesn't leave me a lot to bargain with.'

Repo leaned forward. 'I'm getting the feeling there's more to your story than stumbling on this, publishing it, getting cold feet and deciding to cash in. I might be able to help you. But I need to know what I'm buying. It doesn't do me much good if I make a deal and then a hundred more sequences pop up the next day. I need to understand how a weekend Darkome gene kiddie – no offence – cracks a supposedly uncrackable chip. Assuming that's what you did, and this didn't actually come from the inside. That's the logical explanation, by the way: a security leak. Knowing about that is worth something, too, plugging the leak even more – but you see where I'm coming from? It's not the what, it's the how.'

He laid both hands flat on the table.

'I just work here, OK? I screw this up and Shah will have my guts for garters. You have to give me something, Inara.'

His tone was a little softer. He's been doing this for longer than I've been alive, I reminded myself. It's all negotiation tactics. But Repo's gaze didn't seem to have any guile or deceit in it. I pressed my own palms on the table, deliberately mirroring his gesture. My small hands with their chewed fingernails looked tiny opposite his.

'You might have noticed I'm in PROSPERITY-A,' I said slowly. 'Neoantigen-based real-time cancer prevention.'

Repo nodded.

'You know how it works. Aspis's nanopore sequencer finds cell-free tumour DNA in my blood, sequences it. Your antigen design model in the cloud finds motifs that the immune system can see. The chip makes mRNA to target those. Rinse and repeat, day after day. Works great in theory.

'Except that my mutation rate is much, much higher than normal. If I have a solid tumour, even a tiny one, it can explore pretty much every possible point mutation or combination, all under selective pressure.'

167

Repo's eyes widened.

'I didn't hack your chip,' I said. 'My tumour did.' I rubbed the Heffalump in my armpit.

'Fuck,' Repo breathed. He drummed at the table with his fingers, lost in thought. 'I kept telling her there was going to be a way,' he said to himself. 'There always is.' Then he looked at me again. 'Are you OK?'

'For now. I think.'

'I'll need to see some data. And we'll need to run some tests. But let's say I believe you. So why publish and not get treated immediately? Do you have a death wish?'

'Because I've been living with this for a while and it's cycles and cycles of pain. And because your boss has locked up Aspis so that I can't use it to treat myself. I was going to develop it further, to do a full jailbreak, so I could start testing some ideas. Large scale genome editing. Exosome packaged p53 mRNA with cell entry motifs. Stuff that you don't see coming out of academia because they are too timid. And the drug companies don't care because the market is too small.'

'OK. I get it. So why didn't you go through with it?'

I chewed my lip. 'It doesn't matter. Something got in the way.'

'Who else knows about this?'

Jerome. Svetlana. Now Holst and Mallory. 'No one,' I said, a fraction of a second too late. 'No one who can do anything with it, anyway.' I pointed at the Heffalump. 'You need it – me – to mine more exploits.'

The cat was out of the bag, so I dropped him a data dump of my analysis from the past few days. Repo scanned through it, muttering to himself. After a couple of minutes, he took off his Eyes and rubbed his chin. Then he looked at me.

'You know, this whole thing actually does remind me of a joke,' he said. 'Why did an oncogene start a band?'

I blinked. 'I don't know, why?'

'Because it wanted to make some sick tunes,' he said with a deadpan expression.

I snorted. 'That's terrible.' It really was, but I appreciated the gesture.

'Thank you. I'm here all night. Literally true, thanks to you.' He slumped back in his chair. 'There's more to this, Inara. We'll dig it up. For now, I'll have to go through this with my team.'

'What about the deal?'

Repo got up.

'OK, how about this. You work with us here at Aspis and help us figure out how the hell your cancer is doing this. If this is something that can happen in other Li-Fraumeni patients, it'll be in our interest to kick off a Li-Fraumeni programme ourselves – to seal that loophole, not to mention save a few lives.

'Think of it as a trial period. If we make progress in a couple of weeks, we can talk about full immunity. That's the best I can do at this point, assuming the boss agrees.'

'That's not good enough.' I stood up as well, drawing myself to my full height, still a head short of his. 'I'll co-operate – *if* you agree not to press charges during that trial period. And I can call it quits and leave if I don't agree with what you are doing with the Li-Fraumeni programme, or use whatever you find to directly attack Darkome. All that in a binding contract and it's a deal.'

Repo's flatscreen-mode Eyes pinged and he swiped a notification away. He frowned and moved his mouth as if trying to get rid of a bad taste.

'Fine,' he said. 'We'll get to the paperwork tomorrow. And you stay here on the premises, or no deal. If you are a walking jailbreak, it's too risky to have you running loose.'

I nodded. 'Done.'

Repo huffed. 'I'm going to regret this, aren't I?' He nodded at one of the security guards, a red-haired woman with freckles and light green eyes. 'Lila here will find you somewhere to stay. Get some sleep. We start first thing – assuming this shitshow is over by then.' He waved a hand and lumbered away.

In spite of our situation, I suddenly felt alone and abandoned. It must have shown on my face. Lila said something to the other security guard, a man-mountain with a buzz cut and sharp jawline. He nodded and made his exit as well. Lila waved a hand at me.

'Hi, Inara,' she said, her eyes friendly behind her thick-rimmed Eyes. 'We've got a spot for you a couple of floors up. Unless you'd like something to eat?'

I shook my head. 'I'm fine. Thanks.'

'Suit yourself.' She led me back to the elevators and up. We got out at a floor that looked like a high-end hotel, a corridor with rows of doors. She opened one of them and invited me in.

The room was spacious, with a glossy obsidian desk at one corner. Fancy lighting system with a soft, ambient glow. Floor-to-ceiling windows showed San Francisco's skyline, the lights of high-rises against the dark of the Bay like earthbound constellations. In spite of the luxurious furnishings, it felt impersonal and I suddenly missed my small room in the Haunted House. The one upgrade was a state-of-the-art coffee machine on the marble countertop.

'All right, this is you,' Lila said and popped a contact card into my Eyes. 'Let me know if you need anything.' She gave me a small smile. 'Hey. I probably shouldn't be telling you this, but it's not every day someone stares down Mikko Repo and lives to tell the tale.'

'He seemed to warm up towards the end.' I tried to sound casual, but my heart was still beating faster than normal.

'He only does the stand-up routine if he likes you.'

'That's good to know.' I gave her a curious look. 'Shouldn't you ... I don't know, treat me like a criminal or something? I caused a lot of damage to Aspis, even if I didn't mean for it to happen.'

'Politeness is for free,' Lila said, a touch of chill in her voice. 'Mikko is going to work you hard for whatever you think you're going to get out of this, trust me. My job for now is to make sure you are in shape to do that, mentally and physically.' She shrugged. 'But you've got guts. I respect that. I'd get some rest if I were you.'

She left the room. I sat down on the edge of the plush bed, feeling like I was going to leave stains on the pristine high thread-count sheets. My Senselet had finally gone quiet, and when I checked the Darkome app, there was no network connection. Same for all my messaging apps, and BodyTime. Clearly, Aspis wasn't taking any chances. For all practical purposes, I was a prisoner, even if I was sure they were being careful to stay within legally defensible boundaries.

I plopped down on my back and let my body sink into the mattress. The weight of the night finally crashed down on me. Tears started to well in my eyes. I wanted nothing more than to curl up and cry, to mourn the loss of everything I had worked for over two long years. But Aspis was watching, and there was no room to show weakness. So I held it in, closed the blackout curtains with a whisper, and stared into the formless dark until sleep finally came.

19

Model System

I studied the ghost image of myself hanging in the air in the conference room called Kurri. It was faintly transparent and I could see the ice hockey poster on the wall through it. The data from the PET and MRI scans were all there, a three-dimensional reflection of my insides. The Heffalump was the size of a quarter, a starfish-like shape that clung to the side of my right breast, like one of the mind-controlling parasites of Starro the Conqueror, an enemy of the Justice League.

And then there were the others.

A flowerlike nub in my brain. A fluorescent pool in my liver. A tracery in my right thighbone like moss clinging to a tree, right where my osteosarcoma had been. On and on. Lethal stars and constellations everywhere, in almost every major organ. I had never imagined anything like it, not even in my worst scanxiety nightmares.

The expressions of everyone in the room were serious. Repo, pale and deflated after an all-nighter, on his fourth espresso and toying with a hockey puck. Dr Wu, Senior VP of Oncology, small and neat, beak-nosed, wearing a muted brown pantsuit. Nate Armstrong from the Chip Architecture and Security group had a bulky frame, salt-and-pepper beard and a flannel shirt that made me think of a lumber-jack. Finally, Ellie Martinez from Legal peered at me over her rectangular Eyes. She wore her frizzy silver-streaked hair done up, Bride of Frankenstein style.

'Inara,' Dr Wu said gently, 'this is very unusual. I don't think I've ever seen such a well vascularised network of metastases for a primary tumour in the breast. I understand that we are in a complicated situation here, but I recommend that we come up with an aggressive treatment plan immediately. We should start with a biopsy—'

'No samples,' I said. 'No samples or anything invasive before we have an agreement. No zero-day sequences either.' I did my best to keep my voice firm, even though I felt outside my body, like I was the insubstantial ghost hanging in the air, with everything inside me visible. Death was written all over me in letters made of light, and I couldn't bear to look at it any more.

I took my Eyes off and rubbed my face. I wanted to get away from these strangers with sympathetic faces who were only here because they needed things from me. But I needed things from them.

'Look, Inara—' Repo began.

'Miss Reyes is correct,' Martinez interrupted, enunciating each word precisely. She was the one who had surprised me the most. I had thought she would be my main opponent in negotiations, but instead, she had stood up for me more than once – no doubt protecting Aspis from liability, but still, I appreciated having someone in my corner. 'It is completely up to her if she chooses to provide us with samples of her biological material or not. I sent the latest draft to Amanda this morning. As soon as she signs off on it, Miss Reyes and I will go through it together, and if she is comfortable with it and signs, we can go from there.'

Repo groaned. 'Fine,' he said, leaning back in his chair and tossing the hockey puck up from one meaty hand to the other. 'In the meantime – Nate, what did we get from her chip? Are you happy to discuss that now, Inara? Not invasive, and we have the data anyway.'

I nodded.

Armstrong shifted his thick shoulders. 'Well, something is definitely off. Inara's chip has been burning through re-agent cassettes like there's no tomorrow. Did you notice it needed so many refills?'

'I did. But I thought that's what the neoantigen updates for the trial needed.'

My PROSPERITY-A enrolment had meant that the tiny battery-like things that slotted into the chip's side had been arriving by drone on a regular basis and I had got into a routine of replacing them without thinking. It hadn't even occurred to me that it might be unusual, given that the chip was constantly updating my immune system against the cancer targets that kept popping up in my mutating cells. Now I kicked myself for not having done the maths: the vaccine doses needed should have been tiny.

'What the hell is happening there?' Repo asked. 'Can it be the updates? So many Li-Fraumeni mutations that it keeps pumping them in?'

Nate shook his head. 'The volumes and the synthesis logs don't match up at all. But one of the quality assurance logs

– sequencer instructions to the synthesis chip – was bigger than it should have been. Much bigger.'

'Quality assurance logs?' I asked.

'Right.' Nate glanced at Repo, who nodded. 'Basically, the sequencer has a secondary use: checking the synthesis outputs for accuracy. Accordingly, it has an instruction set that can feed things back to the synthesiser. Something is using that set to tell the synthesiser to make what it wants. The synthesiser is not logging that. But the quality assurance log has a record of all the extra stuff that the chip has been making. This is what I found when I opened it.'

He put his Eyes on and the rest of us followed suit. A list of protein sequences started scrolling in a virtual window in the air. 'I BLASTed them and it's nasty stuff. Immunosuppressive proteins. Decoy antigens. Growth factors. Matrix-degrading enzymes.' The window exploded with annotations and protein structures. 'What's more, they come with the default Aspis localisation tags, targeting different cell types. If you overlay that map on what Dr Wu shared, this is what you get.'

My ghost image lit up like a Christmas tree, with a tracery of bright highways that traversed between the metastases.

'That's incredible,' Dr Wu said. 'The primary tumour has been using the Aspis to make payloads that make it easier to spread around.' She shook her head. 'Sorry. That's too anthropomorphic. It doesn't think or do, it evolves. I've never seen anything like it. Inara, it's a miracle you are not feeling worse. Any headaches? Any other symptoms?'

I swallowed, feeling like a broken piece of hardware. 'No. Wait. Very vivid dreams.'

'You've lost me,' Repo said. 'Nate, did someone hack her Aspis to make her cancer worse?'

'Yeah. The tumour did,' Nate said. 'I have no idea how it's happening, except that it involves the sequencer-synthesis coupling. I'm trying to model the whole thing, but ...' He pointed at me. 'She's the only scaleable model system for this.'

'Inara is a human being and a patient, not a *model system*,' Dr Wu said sharply. 'I'm sorry about this, Inara. I want you to know that we will do everything we can to help you, OK?'

I said nothing. I'd had a master plan for extending the stealth sequences into a full jailbreak. It had involved putting selection pressure on the Heffalump, to force it to do what Nate was describing – I'd keep injecting myself with a tumour suppressor, with the stealth sequence of course, that could be blocked with a specific protein inhibitor that the tumour would be forced to figure out how to make. But while I had been making plans, the Heffalump had done it already. I – we – needed to figure out how.

'What ... what are the treatment options?' I asked Dr Wu.

'Well, we can do a whole range of immunotherapies, biologics and cell therapies. By default, I would resect all the tumours that can be surgically removed, sequence their immune cells and then use Aspis payloads to amplify the natural responses, but here we may have to do it the old-fashioned way. We still have a small manufacturing facility for benchmarking, so that should be possible. It's going to be tough, and this is a *very* strange cancer, but we have options.'

She left the obvious unsaid. If I was actually dying, and

Aspis was the only one who could offer treatments, that was a big negotiation advantage, no matter how unethical it would be to use it. Well, if they wanted to play chicken, I was ready. I had been preparing for this day ever since I was twelve, seen a reminder of it in the mirror every day in my forehead macule and the scar in my thigh.

Or at least that's what I told myself, ignoring the chilly finger running down my spine.

'OK, people. It's in everybody's interests to keep Inara alive,' said Repo. 'Nate, once she co-operates and you get some samples, what's the play here?'

'I think we need to get training data to learn a dictionary between what the tumour sends out and what the synthesiser makes. If Inara is willing, we can set up a little drug delivery implant in her tumour, start perturbing it and see how it responds. We can do some intracellular gene expression recording in parallel. With any luck, we should be able to learn its language. I don't think it's a pattern we can spot – it's probably something really subtle and adversarial, maybe something that breaks the quality assurance neural nets on the chip. It's quite a lot of time in the lab for Inara, though.'

'That's extremely risky,' Dr Wu said. 'We might push it into another evolutionary explosion. I strongly recommend that we—'

'I'll do it,' I said. 'Give me a damn agreement I can sign, and I'll do it.'

'I'd like my objection to this to be noted,' Dr Wu said. 'This is not what I signed up for.' She stood up. 'Do no harm. I think we still believe in that as a company, don't we?'

'Your objection is noted, Doctor,' Repo said. 'As for harm

– it's not Darkome idiots who want to grow a second dick that I'm worried about. Imagine another Decade of Plagues, *except this time we can't stop them, or even see them coming.* We *have* to solve this, or we are all dead in the next couple of years. Do I make myself clear?'

Dr Wu held his gaze for a moment, then nodded. Repo tapped the table with the hockey puck like a judge with a gavel. 'All right, then. Nate, start setting up the data pipeline. I want this fully air-gapped. Let's do it in the Penalty Box. Can you have it ready to go by this afternoon?'

Nate nodded. 'I'll pull in a few RAs from my team to help.'

'No. Do it yourself. Let's keep it in this circle for now.'

'But—'

'You still know how to get your hands dirty, don't you? I'll come and give you a hand.' He turned back to Dr Wu. 'One more thing. How many Li-Fraumeni patients do we have in the PROSPERITY-A trial?'

'There are three others,' she said. 'So far, none of them have exhibited a similar phenotype, but we are watching them.'

Repo frowned. For a moment, I wondered if the p53 mRNA I had helped Mom make had something to do with this. I had effectively been microdosing it during the preps, and it was possible it had accelerated Mom's glioblastoma. But biology was weird, and mine especially was capable of dark miracles on its own: it was possible I would never know.

But, right now I had much more urgent things to worry about.

'All right, folks, good work,' Repo said. 'I would cancel your weekend plans, if I were you. This might take a while.

We should have lunch waiting in the break area, so—'

He never finished the sentence. The door opened, and Amanda Shah walked in.

She seemed smaller in person than in the vircast, a compact dark woman wearing a black North Face jacket and a plain T-shirt. She took her jacket off, put it on the back of a chair and sat down. A tall blonde woman wearing designer Eyes and a golden blazer followed her in, waved at the team and took a seat next to Shah.

'Mikko, catch me up,' Shah said. Repo nodded and flicked her a file, presumably a summary recording of the meeting. Shah stared into her Eyes for a few seconds, then folded them and looked at me. The blonde woman next to her gave me a friendly smile, as if to counterbalance Shah's probing stare.

'I'd like to speak to Inara alone,' Shah said. 'Could you give us a few minutes?'

Repo inclined his head to the rest of the team, and they cleared out, followed by the gold-blazered woman. She shook my hand in passing and whispered, 'I'm Veil. I work with Amanda. We'll talk later, OK?'

Then I was alone with Aspis's founder and CEO.

Shah studied me. I had expected her to be cold and calculating, but her gaze had some warmth, in spite of her poker-faced expression.

'Inara,' she said. 'I have had a trying morning. There have been a number of serious incidents involving your ... stealth sequence. You probably understand this has been quite awkward at a time when we are trying to launch the Panacea Store. I've had a number of tough conversations

180

with shareholders, board members and the media, as well as the families of those affected. Thankfully, no lives were lost, but that was mostly due to luck.'

'Sorry to hear that,' I said. 'I'm having a really awesome morning myself, thank you for asking.'

Shah sighed. 'I am aware of your present difficulties, and I am not trying to blame you. You didn't cause any of this on purpose. And I am truly sorry about your mother. That kind of tragedy is exactly what we are trying to prevent with the Panacea Store.'

'Is it?'

Shah blinked.

'Is it really?' I repeated. 'I listened to the Zephyra Lux hearing. I'm sorry about your aunt, too. But I get the feeling the Panacea Store is ... an excuse. It's not the whole story, is it? And then there is the Z-L Act. God, you really want to control what people like me do with our bodies, don't you?'

'Yes, I do,' she said quietly.

'Why? Because we are not smart enough to make our own decisions? Because we didn't go to Harvard?'

'It's not that.'

'Then help me understand.'

'I don't think we want different things, Inara. I want everyone to be healthy. And I want people to be able to experiment. It's key to our survival as a species. But right now we are on the edge of extinction. Every minute of every single day, I'm terrified that a bad actor, somewhere, has thought of something Aspis hasn't. We got off lightly with the Decade of Plagues. That was architected by some-one who didn't want to kill us – they wanted to slow us down, to keep us occupied. Why exactly, I don't know. The Plagues weren't maximally lethal, merely disruptive. But it's getting easier and easier to create new ones. With Darkome resources, the kinds of people who might become school shooters can now create viruses that could kill billions.'

'But that hasn't happened.'

'No. *Because we have stopped them every time*. Three civilisation-killers in the last two years, detected and dealt with before they spread beyond small outbreaks that were easily contained. All created by non-state actors, small radicalised groups or, in one case, a disturbed individual.'

'Darkome was created to stop the Plagues,' I said. 'We could have contained those outbreaks, too.'

'Maybe. But centralised platforms have advantages here. We share all the data instantly, across three billion Aspis chips, instant human horizontal gene transfer. Darkome will be too slow for the next-generation threats, and is helping to incubate them. We have to find a better way.

'I believe in an expansive human future, Inara. That's what the Panacea Store is about. Safe tools to change human biology, within regulatory frameworks that have guarded us from harm for almost a century, using a unified platform with inbuilt protection from catastrophe.'

'Yeah,' I said. 'So then you create a single point of failure. There are always flaws in any system, and one day, someone worse than me is going to find them.'

'Someone like Dimitry Soloviov?'

I was speechless for a moment.

'We haven't been idle, Inara,' Shah said. 'He is a dangerous man, more so than you know. Ties to post-Putin *siloviki* in Russia, and worse. You did the right thing, coming to us.'

I said nothing. It had been naive to imagine Aspis wouldn't map out every aspect of my life.

'In the world you seem to want, Inara, there is no safety net. Safety does come with some inconvenience, it's true, but isn't a walled garden better than a desert? Wouldn't your mother have wanted you to be safe, with access to a therapy that would have saved her life?'

It was funny how being almost certain that you were going to die made it easier to speak your mind. I leaned back in my chair and folded my arms.

'So you've read my file,' I said, 'and think you know me. But you don't know what it's like to feel powerless, to know your fate has been decided by this alien thing living inside you. Becoming you.

'And then you realise you don't have to believe what doctors tell you, that you can understand what's going on, that there is a whole *community* of people who want to help you. That you can fight. Maybe not win, in the end, but you can fight. With your own hands and your own mind. With your friends by your side. You can be the captain of your ship.

'That's the world I want to live in. My mother died building it. Are you ready to do the same for yours?'

'Yes,' Shah said without hesitation. 'A thousand times, and more.'

Her eyes glimmered. 'When people talk about future generations, they often talk about unimaginably large, abstract numbers. Future humanity in the trillions. But they are not abstract to me. I can ... feel them. If I close my eyes, they are there, waiting to be born, to live their lives, to experience joy and pain and love. And they are relying on us,

183

right now, to make the right decisions, to protect them. I am prepared to make *any* sacrifice for them, and I have, every day of my life since I founded Aspis.'

The conviction in her voice was real, I could feel it. Shah almost had me, then. My chest brimmed with hope for the future.

And then she had to go and spoil it.

'Inara, I do ... respect and try to learn from other ways of thinking. I came here to see if we could work together. I am going to agree to your conditions. And Aspis is going to develop a Li-Fraumeni treatment. That much I can promise. But I have one more request.'

'What's that?'

'Your mother was an influential Darkome figure. If you were to ... make it public that you are working with us, that you are going with the Panacea Store ... well, that could make a difference. Others on Darkome might change their minds about us. Would you think about that?'

Rage built up inside me. I fought it down, squeezed my hands into fists, hard, looked at the conference table's oak surface.

'No,' I said quietly. 'I don't think I will.' I looked up, channelling all the anger into my gaze. 'Any more sugges-tions like that, and I'm walking. Is that understood?'

Shah didn't flinch. 'Understood.'

'What about the Zephyra Lux Act?' I asked. 'Is that going ahead?'

Shah's face hardened. 'It is a necessary tool. Besides, it is out of my hands now. And the latest incidents your exploit triggered are going to win it the support it needs.'

I said nothing. For a moment, my paranoid self wondered

about these *incidents*. The zero-day would have been a perfect excuse for Aspis to frame careless biohackers, exactly like the Zephyra Lux truthers said. Shah's words echoed in my mind. *I am prepared to make any sacrifice.*

I shook my head. Paranoia was not the answer, either, and I didn't really have many options.

'OK,' I said. 'I'll sign. And I'll help you. On one condition.'

'Name it.'

'The Harbour. You try to protect them, when the Act goes through. They can't be the first to be raided. They do Burning Man art, for God's sake. They don't make civilisation-killers. Promise me you'll give them time, and I'll sign.'

'There is no way for me to contractually commit to anything like that—'

'I don't care. Promise. I'll do whatever you want. Just buy them time.'

Quietly, she inclined her head.

'Done,' I said.

Shah offered her hand across the table. I stood up and shook it. Her grip was dry and smooth and strong.

'All right,' I said, sitting back down, suddenly tired and empty. 'I'm ready for the legal lady now.'

Shah took her jacket, nodded, and left the room. And then I was alone with my ghost again.

20

The Penalty Box

I spent the next hour with Ellie the lawyer, going through the contract while munching on a grain bowl. The local copy of Donnie the AI running in my Eyes summarised the key points. It was surprisingly benign, although I didn't love the restrictions on my movements during the so-called trial period.

We were about halfway through when Veil – the blonde woman with the golden blazer, Amanda's chief of staff, as it turned out – breezed in with a cardboard tray of coffees.

'Hi!' she said. 'I'm going to sit in, if you guys don't mind, and shadow Inara for a bit. Amanda wants to know as soon as you make progress.' She sat down, and fiddled with her Eyes in touchscreen mode. Her fingernails were painted white and immaculately manicured. I accepted the coffee gratefully and continued. Occasionally, I noticed Veil looking at me. She immediately turned her luminous smile on, but there was an unease in her expression that I thought I recognised from waiting for scans: worrying about something that was about to happen. Given what Shah had said, it wasn't surprising. Clearly, Aspis was playing a high stakes game that I only caught tiny glimpses of.

Finally, we were done. I signed an actual honest-to-god dead tree printout of the contract, and Ellie gave me a copy. I was now technically an Aspis consultant, working for them as an independent contractor.

Then it was time to get to work. Dr Wu came to pick me up, and took me to the floor with the oncology lab where my scans had been done that morning. This time, I lay down while a sinuous robot arm carried out several extremely precise biopsies, which hurt less than an acupuncture needle.

The final step was implanting the drug delivery device Nate had been talking about. Dr Wu showed it to me: it was essentially an implantable, dumber version of the Aspis chip that had an external port for mRNA or drug delivery. She used a local anaesthetic and installed it via laparoscopic surgery. Her serious face was impassive but there was a visible tension and annoyance in her eyes.

We also discussed my treatment plan. Assuming I got through the next few days, the following months would be rough, with regular infusions of genetically engineered immune cells and an mRNA-encoded cocktail of biologic immunotherapies. Normally, I would have loved to nerd out about Dr Wu's proposal to use CAR-NK cells as opposed to CAR-Ts. She felt that NKs, or natural killer cells, might be less vulnerable to Heffalump manipulation. I wasn't sure I agreed after what Nate had shared in the conference room. We were going to be fighting a cyberwar with sticks and stones. But the earnestness of her concern was comforting after the intense day, and I mostly listened, letting Donnie take notes, and pretended to be a good patient.

Dr Wu was explaining another idea of combining CAR-NKs with bispecific antibodies, when Veil knocked on her office door.

'Sorry. I don't mean to interrupt, Inara, but Nate and Mikko are ready for you in the Penalty Box.' Veil flashed a cheery smile, but her eyes held a flicker of unease.

Dr Wu frowned. 'Well, actually—'

'It's fine,' I said. 'We can go. The Penalty Box?'

'Air-gapped lab. The most secure place in the whole building.' The corners of Veil's mouth strained ever so slightly. 'It's really cool. You'll see!'

The three of us wandered through the busy floor, down a series of corridors past open-plan office space and labs, to a reinforced door which Veil unlocked with a retinal scan. The large space inside was a little chilly, with light blue walls, and it was without a doubt the best equipped lab I had ever seen. In spite of the fact that I was going to be the subject of an experiment here, I wandered through it in a daze, ran my fingers along a gleaming bench that held an atomic force microscope, and stared at a high throughput BioSynth gene synthesiser. A series of rails connected most benches, with a forest of robot arms sliding along them, moving ninety-six-well plates around in and out of centrifuges and pipetting into them using a variety of attachments.

If there was a genre of molecular biology porn that hadn't been subsumed by Illusia yet, this place deserved an adult industry award. It wasn't completely cold and inhuman, either: the whiteboards that covered one wall had hockey stick and puck shaped magnets, photos of people with their kids, and a weird dried-up marker drawing of what looked like a dog wearing a skirt, perhaps a memento from a particularly weird brainstorming session. There were no windows, but there was a large screen next to the entrance that showed a view of the main break area, presumably via a CCTV link since the whole place was in a Faraday cage.

Veil grinned at me. 'You should have seen where Aspis started out. Our first lab was inside a shipping container in an old chocolate factory in West Berkeley. One time, it had been used for a rave, and we had investors coming for a morning meeting. Amanda called me at 5.30 a.m. and we went in to clean up and scrub the floors. She still had yellow rubber gloves on when they arrived.' She smiled a little sadly at the memory. 'Good times.'

Repo and Nate were huddled next to an inclined chair setup and a bench which was a familiar explosion of chaos in the pristine setting: a cell sorter, a large high-throughput nanopore, equipment I didn't recognise – and a QENF node in its own supercooled pillar, a quantum neural processor, an example of the breakthrough that Soloviov had been so worried about.

'Hi, Inara!' Nate said brightly. 'Are you up for a session for an hour or so? Shouldn't take longer than that.'

'Sure,' I said. 'Do your worst.' Dr Wu flinched at that.

Repo looked at me. 'Deal is a deal.' He held out a hand. 'Let's have them.'

I nodded, and passed him the file containing the rest of the stealth sequences. He grunted, although whether out of displeasure or satisfaction I couldn't be sure. Then he glanced at his watch, a cheap plastic thing with an old-fashioned digital display. 'I need to step out to get another update going to cover these, ,' he said. 'You kids have fun.'

There is a theory about categories of fun. Type I fun is

the kind of fun you enjoy while doing it – pizza or sex. Type II fun is terrible while it's happening, but makes for a great story afterwards, like being chased by a bear. Nate's effort to map out how exactly the Heffalump was doing the jailbreak was Type III: not fun. I lay on the dentist-style inclined chair, sensor bands wrapped around my head, chest and stomach. I had one tube going into the drug implant port in the Heffalump, and a mosquito-style device sampling my blood.

Nate routed the samples in real time through a cell sorter and a nanopore sequencer, assisted by the ubiquitous robot arms. Dr Wu hovered next to me and monitored my vitals through her Eyes. I had mine on, too, but the data stream was too much to take in. The number of things on me and in me was overwhelming, and the Heffalump pulsed with pain following each new mRNA or small molecule perturbation Nate pumped in.

I lost sense of time in the misery. At some point, Repo returned and joined the small group standing around me. The sensory overload became white noise, and I developed a pounding headache. I closed my eyes and tried to imagine being on a boat in a vast ocean, where each flush of nausea, pinch or headache pulse was a wave, washing over me, no difference between them and my breathing or my thoughts, all with the same taste.

Finally, it was over. I opened my eyes, blinking at the LED lights, aching everywhere.

'You did really well, Inara,' Dr Wu said. 'Your heart rate is really high, so I'm going to get you a sedative to calm you down a bit, OK?'

I nodded. My mouth was dry, and I asked for water. Repo

handed me a plastic bottle, and I drank it in one go. Dr Wu was rummaging through her medical kit, when a female voice spoke through an intercom speaker. 'Dr Wu, you are needed on the thirty-eighth floor, please.'

'I'll be right back,' she said. 'No more of this today, OK?' she told Nate. 'She needs some rest.'

Nate nodded. 'I think we got enough input-output pairs to put something meaningful together. With any luck, we'll have a mapping from circulating RNA transcripts to chip state and synthesis outputs, and then we are not far from mechanism.

'I'm betting it's a nanopore version of the buffer overflow attack. The nanopore outputs a waveform that we analyse with a model on a neuromorphic chip. I suspect the ... Heffalump is doing something adversarial to that model that gets it to output data that overflows a memory location that then executes code to talk to the synthesiser. It's clever as hell. Like a magic trick.'

'Cancer is clever,' Dr Wu said. 'It's us. Or, rather, a better version of us. A dark twin.'

'Mukherjee,' I said.

She smiled. 'We're going to talk about that when I come back. Won't be long.' She headed out through the security door, which closed behind her with a hiss.

While Repo and Nate started analysing the data, I used the restroom and did another gawking tour of the Penalty Box. Veil was sitting on a high chair next to one of the lab benches, eyes closed, breathing deeply. She opened one eye when I approached.

'Sorry to disturb you,' I said.

'No worries. I was almost done anyway. It's so quiet here.

191

I don't often get a chance to meditate.' To me, she didn't look like someone who had glimpsed enlightenment. Her expression was calm, but she kept scratching her thumbnail with the nail of her forefinger, and had worn away some of the white lacquer. 'Don't tell Amanda, but I sometimes come here just to be properly offline.'

'Labs are like that,' I said. 'Calm. You can't hurry biology. There's a lot of waiting. I love labs.'

Veil smiled sadly. 'You do, don't you? You belong here.' She looked around the lab. 'It's good to figure that out early in life. I had many twists and turns on the way. Some regrets, but it all worked out in the end.'

She stood up, stretched and suddenly frowned. 'What's going on there?' She pointed at the large display next to the security door, with the view of the break area.

Two people in the middle of the break area were staring at each other: a large African American man and a dark-haired heavyset woman. They had nearly identical expressions – wide eyes, shock and fear. The man pointed at the woman and shouted something inaudible. There was commotion around them. A chair flew through the air and crashed against the window.

Repo and Nate joined us. Mikko went to the wired intercom panel next to the screen. 'Security. This is Repo. What the hell is going on in there?' There was no response. 'Hello?'

Then the screen started blinking with a warning. POTENTIAL BIOHAZARD OR BIOWEAPON. A calm voice spoke through the intercom.

'*Attention all Aspis personnel, this is an urgent announcement. Our biohazard detection system has identified a potential biohazard or bioweapon threat within the facility. For your safety and the safety of others, we are initiating our emergency response protocol, effective immediately.'*

'*Voi vitun saatanan perkele*,' Repo swore. 'If this is a drill, I'm going to have someone's head.'

'No drills,' Veil said. 'I would have known.' She pulled out her folded Eyes, glanced at the screen, and snapped it shut in frustration. We were still in a Faraday cage.

I felt weightless. The world was plunging into chaos again, and I had nothing solid to hold on to. Anxiety filled my chest like an expanding balloon, and I started doing boxed breathing.

'*Please remain calm and follow these instructions*,' droned the intercom. Repo tapped at a panel. 'No. Definitely real.'

'*One. Cease all ongoing activities and secure any sensitive materials or equipment—*'

Repo slammed a ham-sized fist on the wall screen. 'I can't do shit from here, that's the whole point. Fuck.'

'*If you are in an affected area, the hermetically sealed doors will close automatically. Do not attempt to leave the area or force open any sealed doors.*'

'Mikko?' Nate asked. 'Mikko, are you all right?'

'*—proceed immediately to your designated safe zone, following the emergency exit signs and avoiding any sealed areas—*'

'What do you mean, of course I am—'

The big engineer's eyes were wide and his gaze flickered from Repo to me and Veil with a growing look of absolute terror. He backed away from us towards the nearest lab bench. 'Don't ... don't come any closer,' he said hoarsely. 'I don't know what you are, but stay away from me. Stay away.' He grabbed a metal rod that might have been a robot arm part and brandished it.

'Please remember that your safety is our top priority. Our specialised hazmat teams and robotic units are being deployed to assess the situation and initiate decontamination. We are collaborating with external agencies to ensure a coordinated response.'

Repo took a step forward, arms raised non-threateningly. 'Nate, it's me, it's Mikko, honest to God, mate. Something is messing with your head. This is an attack on Aspis. We're not the enemy. You're not well. Put that thing down and let me help you, OK?'

He took another step, and Nate snapped.

The big engineer swung the metal rod in a skull-crushing blow. Repo stepped aside with an agility that belied his bulk. One of his arms snaked around Nate's neck in a choke hold and tightened. Nate roared, bent forward and almost lifted Repo off the ground. Then he threw himself back, slamming the chief security officer against a bench. Repo grunted but held on. I looked around for a weapon, but the two men were rolling on the floor. Nate clawed at Repo's hands and drew blood. Repo rolled onto his back, locked his hold with his other hand, and squeezed. Nate's face turned blue. He made a gurgling sound. Then his eyes rolled back, and he went limp.

Repo sat up slowly, cradling Nate's head. He was breathing hard and his chest heaved. His face was beetroot red.

'Stay calm and follow all protocols. We will provide regular updates as more information becomes available. Thank you for your cooperation.' The intercom looped back to the beginning.

'Tie ... him ... up,' he grunted, waving a hand. 'Zip ties ... utility drawer.' Veil was already opening a storage unit on wheels and rummaging through it.

I shook all over and my knees wobbled. I leaned on a lab bench and stared at Nate's still form on the floor.

'It's Zemyevit Disease, right?' I said. 'But weaponised, with a stealth sequence, so it's not triggering an Aspis response. It's Soloviov.' The three of us might have it too, I realised, Svetlana's story and the scar in her ear flashing through my mind. Potentially dying from cancer was one thing, but losing myself utterly to weaponised paranoia was way worse.

Repo spat a gob of blood on the floor and glared at me. The firmware update process to update Aspises and whatever sequencers the company used for biohazard detection hadn't been quick enough. If I'd handed them over faster—

'I didn't know,' I whispered. 'I'm sorry.'

Repo got up slowly and carefully, clutching at his lower back. 'It doesn't matter now,' he said. 'We have bigger problems.' Veil handed him a bunch of zip ties and he secured Nate's feet. 'Zemyevit Disease?' she asked. 'Do I want to know?'

'One of the nastier Plagues,' Repo muttered. 'Turns everyone else into pod people in your eyes, makes you violent.' He rolled the unconscious engineer on his side and tied the man's hands. 'Might be on some improved backbone with rapid onset of symptoms, given the timing. It must have got in in the last twenty-four hours.' His head jerked up and he stared at me. 'What did I say about social engineering bullshit?'

My heart missed a beat.

'It's not me. There's no way,' I said. 'The timing doesn't work. I only gave Soloviov the sequences shortly before I came here. He could not have infected me then. It must have taken at least a few hours to synthesise the virus.'

Repo narrowed his eyes. 'Well, excuse me if I don't take your word for it.'

'And how come I don't have any symptoms?'

'Pre-treatment with an inhibitor to whatever set of viral proteins drives the phenotype,' he said. 'Perfect Typhoid Mary.'

Veil touched Repo's arm. 'Are *you* feeling OK? That's sounding like ... well, paranoia.'

Repo let out a barklike laugh. 'Ha! I was born this way.'

'Either way, we should evacuate, right?' Veil said. 'Full transfer of all unexposed key personnel to the Arc, isn't that the protocol?' Her elfin face was anxious. 'Amanda needs me, and I'd say Inara counts as essential personnel right now.'

Repo shook his head. 'I wrote the protocol, remember? I would say the three of us are pretty fucking exposed right now, even in the best case scenario that we don't have patient zero right here with us. We should stay here at least until the decontamination units arrive. I don't want to sit here on my ass any more than you do.' He pointed at the screen. Panicked figures ran across it every now and then, a young man in a T-shirt pursued by security in respirator masks. 'Those are my people out there. But the smart play is to stay put.'

Veil held his gaze, folding her arms. 'I disagree. We should—'

'Stop it, you two,' I said. Repo's accusations had made me angry, hot and fast. 'If *only* there was *some way* to figure out if we are infected or not.' I gestured at the world-class molecular biology lab around us with all its humming equipment. 'Who wants to go first?'

21

The Jailbreak

The assay took ten minutes. All it needed was a command to the Penalty Box's AI to design and run the protocol, and nasal, saliva and blood samples from the three of us. We had the stealth sequences and the original Zemyevit sequence from Aspis's files, so making PCR primers with the oligo synthesiser was no problem. I watched the robot arms move around on the rails and dance, mesmerised. I had given the Box a hard time constraint, and it ended up using the atomic force microscope on a simple PCR reaction to get a faster readout. The results flashed on a virtual screen in our Eyes.

We were all positive.

It really wasn't my day when it came to medicine.

Repo regarded the two of us warily. 'It might be many hours before we get out of here,' he said. 'The response teams are not going to rush in. We ran some drills where the exposed are aggressive and uncooperative. They'll have to contain them one by one.'

'Couldn't they gas everyone or something?' I asked.

Repo shook his head. 'If we had designed the HVAC system to allow delivery of a pharmacological agent ... well, then we'd have had an HVAC system that could be used to deliver a pathogen or a toxin. No, this is going to be slow. And some of our security people have access to weapons. So ...' He let his voice trail off.

'We try to leave, we get attacked,' I said. 'We stay here, we attack each other.'

'Right,' Repo said.

'I still think risking it to get out is the best option,' Veil said. 'We can run for it. The Arc will have facilities to treat us.'

Repo scratched his beard.

'I'd propose zip ties for everyone, but the last person would have to somehow secure themselves. We could try to get a robot to do it, but I'm not sure we can bypass all the safety protocols. Or there's that.' He pointed at the open medical kit Dr Wu had left on a bench top. 'Neurocin. One of us injects the other two, then themselves.'

'Can the infected get in somehow?' I asked. 'I don't want to be lying here helpless.'

Repo grunted. 'There's at least half a dozen people in my team out there with access. But that's a risk we might have to take.'

'Or one of us might be pretending not to be affected right now,' Veil said darkly, 'and then deal with the other two when they are unconscious.'

'That doesn't track with the symptoms we've seen, but it's not impossible,' Repo admitted. 'How are you both feeling? '

Veil rubbed her forehead. 'I'm a little warm. But I might be imagining it.' She sat down and buried her face in her hands. 'Fine. Give me the syringe. I'll do it.' Then she looked up. 'Wait. Do we know if the ... Zemyevit has any permanent effects? I don't want to go to sleep and wake up someone else.'

'I heard the people with the original strain mostly recovered,' I said. Less so the people close to them, I thought, but kept my mouth shut. I told the local Donnie copy in my Eyes to look up the Zemyevit mechanism and shuddered. Neurotoxins targeting facial recognition, emotional processing, dopaminergic system – it could well have at least some permanent effects.

'That tracks,' Repo said. 'How about you, Inara?'

'I feel fine,' I said. 'Except for, you know.' Mikko nodded. I thought of Svetlana, and how she had lived through an entire country with this thing. No wonder she was such a badass –

Then it clicked. *She had lived through it without getting it.*

'Antibodies,' I said. 'We can make antibodies.'

'How?' Repo said. 'I mean, sure, the standard pan-Plagues countermeasure library on the Aspis has some against the original, but this is something new.'

He opened a virtual screen in our Eyes and pulled up the Zemyevit we had PCR'd out of our own samples, contrasting it against the Zemyevit sequence on file. 'It's not the original Bulgarian strain. The Aspis protein design model could probably generate an *in silico* design from the sequence, but we can't access it from here.'

I rubbed the macule on my forehead. 'Soloviov only had hours to put this together. I bet it's a dirty hack and he simply changed the cell entry receptor or something. That's what I would have done.'

I told the Box to query the open reading frames – the

proteins the virus made – from its local metagenomic database. And there it was.

'There we go. It's using a tweaked protein from something called the Powassan virus to get into cells. Super rare, you get it from tick bites sometimes, but it leads to a brain infection. Aaaand there is a published antibody sequence. High affinity, too.'

'Great,' Repo said. 'Now we know that Soloviov is lazy and tick bites suck. Don't get me wrong, as soon as we get out of here and to the Arc, we can roll out an update to everyone and stop this thing. But how's that going to help us right now?'

'Are you kidding?' I held up my arm. 'We have Aspises! We throw in the Powassan antibody sequence and have the chips make the mRNA. Boom. Instant immunity.'

Repo scratched his beard. 'Can't. We'll need hardware keys for the chips' synthesisers, and we don't have any here. For—'

'For safety,' I said bitterly. 'Right. OK. We could run an *in vitro* transcription reaction here, manually. We have all the gear. Except—' Except that it would take hours, and we would all be at each other's throat by then. There had to be a better way.

And of course, there was. In spite of the network of metastases in my body, the virus pumping neurotoxins into my brain, I found myself grinning at Repo.

'Well, in that case,' I said, 'I guess we have to jailbreak them.'

*

The chaos outside the lab continued. We tried not to look at the screens as we worked. Someone banged on the security door with a fire extinguisher.

I had originally guessed the synthesis jailbreak – not merely hiding sequences from Aspis, but reprogramming it to make any mRNA I wanted – would take months of cranking with full Soloviov infinite budget support. We had maybe an hour. I had chills and the beginnings of a head-ache, and this time it wasn't just my imagination.

We had the Box's QENF model go through the data Nate and Repo had sucked out of the Heffalump and my blood-stream earlier. It pieced together a map of the sequencer and synthesis chip's state as a function of sequence inputs. I soon got lost in the high-dimensional data visualisation blooming into being around us, but Repo seemed at home navigating it.

'Looks like Nate was right,' he said. 'It's adversarial: it's messing up the outputs of the neuromorphic chip on the sequencer that converts the nanopore signal into a se-quence, and that leads to a buffer overflow. Which gets you executable code in the sequencer's memory. And then you can have it instruct the synthesis chip through the quality assurance API. It's brilliant.' His expression was grim, but there was a mischievous look in his eyes, like a little boy dismantling a toy. 'I told those idiots we'd find zero-days, sooner or later.' He looked at me. 'OK, Inara. What next?'

'Let's hook the chip to our Eyes via Bluetooth. It can talk to peripherals, right?'

'Sure, but that would mean registering an app in the App Store, and getting an API key from—' He grimaced. 'Let me guess. You have jailbroken Eyes.'

'Yup. They'll run anything. You should come to the dark side, Mikko.'

He raised his eyebrows.

'What makes you think I haven't been there?'

It did take a couple of actual minutes of the quantum neural processor time to churn out a set of sequences that encoded the software we wanted. It occurred to me that I would never have been able to do this on my own, with or without Darkome support.

While the gene synthesiser was printing the jailbreak sequences, I prompted Donnie to write an app that could talk to Aspis. I added a search for public Darkome libraries – good thing I always cached a local copy – and some of my own bookmarks. We weren't necessarily planning to deliver more than one sequence, but it was hacker second nature to overbuild to solve the fully generalised version of any problem. I felt a pang of regret that I wouldn't be able to spend a few weeks trying every cool biohack I'd ever come across – not to mention trying to figure out how to tackle the Heffalump using more aggressive means than what Dr Wu was proposing.

In a few minutes, the jailbreak DNA cocktail was ready. I mixed it in saline buffer: we didn't have to do fancy de-livery. A transdermal injection was enough for the Aspis nanopore to pick it up, and it only needed a few molecules.

I did the injections, starting with Repo's hairy, burly arm, right next to his black base model Aspis. To my surprise, he flinched when I moved the needle close to his skin.

'Sorry. Hate needles. Always have.' He looked away and closed his eyes. I pinched a fold of his flesh close to the injection site and slid the needle in.

'Is it done?' he asked, opening one eye. I gave him a sympathetic smile and patted his shoulder. 'It's done. You are back on the dark side.'

Veil had a high-end Aspis, with a gold enamelling pattern and a tiny gem insert. She smiled through it, but did a quick intake of breath when the needle went in.

And finally, me. The bite of the needle was a false promise, I knew, a dream fulfilled only to be taken away. But for a few moments, I would truly be unleashed at last.

I held my breath while the app in my Eyes searched for the Bluetooth connections. One by one, the devices popped up as long hexadecimal IDs.

'OK,' I said. 'We are in business. Here it comes.'

I copypasted the monoclonal antibody sequence in the window, specified the mRNA architecture (linear), add-ons (maximum translation speed), and the amount. One hundred micrograms of mRNA should do it. I hit the 'send' button, and the tiny mRNA factories we were all wearing swung into action. I could see the enzymatic synthesis chip churning out the DNA template that got guided into microfluidic channels, encountering polymerases which copied it onto many mRNA strands, that got shepherded through narrow passages to eliminate any impartial or folded copies; the capping process that added protective ends to the molecules; the pre-made helper mRNAs that would get the target muscle cells to produce vesicles that would package the main mRNA and ferry it where it was most needed. The Aspis felt warm, suddenly, and the skin around it ached.

'It's heating up. Is this normal?' Veil asked, massaging her Aspis. 'Did it malfunction?'

Nate's chip model was still open, and I fed the logfile

stream from our Aspises into it. It explained that all chips were functioning within normal parameters, but that the amount of mRNA being made was greater than what was usually required for vaccine-style antigen updates, and that was causing the warming.

'How will we know if it worked or not?' Veil asked.

'Our viral loads will go down,' I said. 'We can run the assay again in an hour or so. It will take a little time for the antibody levels to ramp up. Also, if we don't start going for each other's throat in that time, something is working.'

Repo looked thoughtful. 'OK. If this does work, we do need to push it out to everyone, at least in this local area. I can do it from the backup facility at the Arc. Once the antibodies have kicked in, I'm going to make a run for it.' He pointed at the screen. 'It's looking quieter now, and I think I can make it to the elevators.'

'Shouldn't we all go?' I asked. 'Maximises the chances of at least one of us getting there.'

'I agree,' Veil said, a steely look in her eyes. 'We can't let you do this alone.'

'Inara, think this through,' Repo said. 'If this is Soloviov and not some random Darkome nutter, he is doing this for a reason. As you said, this wasn't a well-designed virus. It's meant to achieve something – like, for example, force us to get you out of the building or to cover a kidnapping attempt. That's what I would do. So it's absolutely necessary that both of you stay put.'

Frustrated, I stared at the screen, at the cracked window and the disarray of furniture. A motionless human form lay prone on the floor on the edge of the view, and I wondered if they were still alive. Was this my fault? So far, the

Heffalump had been a curse, not only for me but for those around me. I thought about the path from the disappearance of my oncosense to here, and wished I had never taken the first step.

It was at that moment that Veil plunged the syringe full of Neurocin into Repo's neck.

His eyes rolled. He opened his mouth to say something, but then a wave of confusion washed over his face and he toppled to the ground.

I stared at Veil. The antibody levels hadn't gone up quickly enough. She had to be infected. But the anguished look on her face was not madness.

'I'm sorry, Inara,' she said. 'You are going to have to come with me.'

Part Four

The Dark Road, 2041

22

Mirror Neurons

'You ... you are with Soloviov,' I gasped. 'Screw you. I'm not going anywhere.' The adrenaline made my mind fast and clear. I eyeclicked on the Aspis app. There had to be a payload I could get her Aspis to make to disable her. She was bent over Repo's still form, rummaging through his pockets, and I was maniacally trying to think of a search term—

'I knew it,' she said, pulling out a small pistol from Mikko's jacket. She clicked the safety open and pointed it at me. 'Take your Eyes off,' she said. 'If I feel anything coming through the Aspis, you're dead. I'd tear it off, but I have to wear it to get through the security doors. But make no mistake. I only need a large enough tumour sample. The rest of you is optional. Up to you.'

I eyeclicked on the only thing in the jailbreak app's default view I could see that made any sense. Then I removed my Eyes, slowly. Veil held out her hand. I folded them and gave them to her, praying quietly. My knees almost gave out, but the anger saved me again, flaring up in my chest and clearing out the fear.

I pointed at Mikko. 'He had better be alive, or you *will* have to drag me out dead.'

Veil looked at Mikko a little regretfully. 'He should be fine,' she said. 'It's hard to overdose on Neurocin, although a very high dose gives you a few hours of complete amnesia. So once we torch this place, your jailbreak leaves with us.'

Keeping the small snub-nosed gun trained at me, she glanced at the wallscreen. 'Penalty Box immolation protocol,' she said. 'Authorisation: Veil Montgomery, Chief of Staff.'

Immediately, the robot arms started moving, grabbing samples, moving biowaste containers. The lights on all the instruments came on, as if they had all been possessed. The quantum neural processor's covering frosted up as liquid nitrogen escaped with a hiss.

'Complete data purge, down to security cameras,' Veil said. 'It's sometimes convenient to have a truly paranoid chief security officer.'

'Why are you doing this? You've been with Shah from the start. Do you mean that all this time—'

'That doesn't matter now, Inara. I'd think about your next move very carefully, if I were you. You wouldn't want anything to happen to your father, for example. If I don't deliver you to a safe location in the next three hours, well—'

'Why should I believe you?'

'Soloviov does not bluff, you should know that by now. Come on. We need to get out of here.'

She grabbed my arm, pressed the nose of the pistol into my ribs and started towards the security door.

It opened, we walked through, and then we were in hell. The corridors echoed with cries of pain and terror. A woman huddled in the corner of a conference room, hugging her knees and shaking. Her hands were covered in blood. There were three other people in the room, slumped in chairs. One had empty eye sockets. In a restroom, a man was beating the mirror with bloody fists, over and over and over, screaming. There were distant gunshots.

There had been a time soon after Mom died when the intensity of the daily grief and my anger at Dad had pushed me into a strange place where no normal emotion could reach. Time had slowed down to a crawl, and I had operated on autopilot. This was like that. I could not understand what I was seeing, and allowed Veil to lead me on.

We passed through the breakroom. The ice hockey memorabilia display cases were shattered. The kitchen drawers were open. *Someone has knives*, I thought.

We turned a corner into a corridor leading to the elevators. An Aspis scientist with a Led Zeppelin T-shirt charged at us with a raised hockey stick. I tried to pull away to dodge, but Veil held me with an iron grip. She raised the gun and shot the man in the leg. He fell to the ground, screaming. We kept walking. The elevator doors should have been sealed, but they opened for Veil. My stomach fell as we plummeted through the Spire's translucent interior, scenes of fighting and horror all around, a terrible, dark panopticon. Then we were underground. The doors opened to an expansive parking garage. After the screams, the silence was deafening. A large, custom self-drive SUV waited a few yards away. The doors lifted open, Veil herded me in, and they closed again with a hermetic hiss.

The car accelerated up a ramp. The windows dimmed. Veil and I sat across from each other. There were plush seats for six in the roomy interior, three facing three, with a low table and a touchscreen in the middle. The screen lit up, showing a map to the car's destination: somewhere in the Santa Clara Mountains, fifty miles south of the city.

Veil took off her mask and grabbed a water bottle from a small drinks cabinet. She tossed me one as well, opened hers with her teeth and took a sip.

I pressed the bottle against my forehead. I didn't have fever, and the antibodies were probably working, but the cool plastic was a physical sensation I could focus on instead of the turmoil of fear and anger inside my head.

'Where are we going?' I asked. I didn't really need to know, the plan was clear. There was an offsite backup facility in the mountains; we would get intercepted on the way. Everything Veil had done so far had plausible deniability with the Zemyevit Disease in play, even shooting the infected man with the hockey stick. She might even be able to insert herself back into Aspis, once I was in Soloviov's hands.

She said nothing. Maybe my desperate attempt to gain an advantage by having her Aspis express something had been in vain. The only thing that had been accessible within a fraction of a second had been the LuxLives project – an empathy-enhancing payload. Maybe it could help Veil to understand my point of view.

I wasn't sure how long it would take to have an effect, assuming it worked in the first place. It was a cool design, though. Mirror neuron specific mRNA circuits for AMPA receptors and the stargazin protein – named after the effect it had in mice – packaged in brain-targeting exosomes. In theory they would combine to make mirror neurons in Veil's brain hyper-responsive, almost immediately after mRNA reached them.

I tried to do the maths in my head: maybe thirty minutes to get from circulation into the brain? Longer? Minutes per protein molecule to get made in the neurons? It could work now, tomorrow or never.

I had to keep her talking.

'I still don't understand,' I said. 'What does Soloviov have on you? What about Shah? I mean, I disagree with her on most things, but at least she is not a fucking mass murderer.'

Veil's left hand – the one not holding the gun – twitched. She picked at her thumbnail with a hooked index finger, making a faint scraping sound, audible over the faint hum of the car's engine.

'It's better you don't talk,' she said.

I ignored her. 'Seriously. Are you an AI doomer extremist? Is that it? Or he's blackmailing you? You are married, right?' I pointed at the golden ring on her left hand. 'I mean, why not tell me at this point? I'm not going to judge. Any more than I already have.'

I let my anger show, and saw it immediately reflected on her face. She lunged across the table, cocked the gun and pressed it right into my forehead macule. Its tiny metal pucker pressed hard on my skin. 'Shut. Up,' she hissed into my ear. 'Not. One. More. Word.'

I took a shuddering breath and nodded. She retreated back into her seat and slumped down, but the gun was still vaguely pointed in my direction. We sat in silence for a while.

My heartbeat settled back down and my bladder stopped aching. Had it been half an hour already since I triggered her

Aspis with the LuxLives payload? I wasn't sure. Veil might have mirrored my anger — or the stress of double-crossing one colleague and shooting another was getting into her.

There was only one way to find out. Very slowly, I put a hand on my right knee.

After a couple of seconds, Veil did the same.

I tried to remember what I knew about mirror neurons. There was a process called neural resonance: if you saw someone in pain, mirror neurons fired the same neural circuits that would come online if you were experiencing that pain yourself. Emotional contagion.

I could try to get Veil to feel something by making myself feel it. But I couldn't fake it. Not that I'd be able to, anyway: I had never been much of an actor. Fear would be easy. I was scared shitless. But fear could trigger violence. No, it had to be something softer, positive. When had I felt like that?

I thought about the Mount Tam picnic two and a half years ago.

The climb up the mountainside, along a forest path with worn tree roots like steps, bubbling streams and respite from the heat. Stumbling across rocks in the final bit to the summit, to meet the view of Golden Gate and all of the Bay painted across the horizon. I let the memory fill me, warm and golden, and spoke again.

'Hey, Veil. You must be feeling pretty good about yourself right now.'

She said nothing. Her blue eyes were wary.

'I mean, you don't have to lie anymore. You get to be yourself. Everything's changed. The future is wide open.'

Did her gaze soften, just a touch?

'I remember how that felt,' I said. 'It was when my mom and I saw her tumour DNA counts going down. She was responding to to the p53 therapy we'd made. We had a picnic with Dad to celebrate. Cheap champagne. We were so happy.'

Veil smiled. She had a partner, a family maybe. She had to have some good memories, no matter what Soloviov had done to her. I held on to the images from my own past. Champagne up my nose, the wind tugging at the blanket's corners. Dad standing up and spreading his arms and whooping. I squeezed the moment into a glowing diamond in my chest. Tears welled in my eyes. Veil leaned back in her seat, tension gone from her shoulders.

'Lila,' she whispered. Her gun hand rested on the seat. I only had to lunge forward and grab it—

And then my memory rushed forward and fucked it up.

We settled down in the champagne afterglow and ate. Mom said she wanted us to decide what to do as a family, but that she wanted to stay in the Harbour, even if the cure worked. That she felt like we belonged there. Dad froze, a cracker with cheese halfway into his mouth. He put it down and said he'd have to think about that. Mom hugged herself and looked at him quietly, waiting. Something passed between them. Dad got up, said he needed to take a short walk. I started after him, but Mom took my arm.

'Let him go, peixinha,' she said. 'He needs to find his own way to us.'

I got up anyway and pulled away from her delicate grip. 'He won't,' I said. 'But I will make him.'

Somewhere, Veil growled. I tried to fight back the memory

215

of anger, but it was already on my face, in my curled-up fists.

Reflected in the black hole of the gun's barrel, pointed at my face.

'It was you, you little bitch,' Veil hissed. 'You did this. I was doing everything he wanted, everything she wanted, at the same time. I was going to make her see. And if she didn't, give him what he needed so he would. I couldn't tell Lila. I couldn't tell the kids. But it was all for them. I was making it work for them.

'And then you. Burn it all, he said, for this one little girl, for her tumour. After everything I had done. Well, guess what? I'm going to make sure you burn too.'

Her face was a terrible mask. Her knuckles were white. This was it. No way out. The clarity felt good. The gun's black hole swallowed all my fear.

Only light remained. In an instant, it burned through all my lies. That I didn't know why Mom had died. That it was all Dad's fault. That I needed to let the Heffalump grow to beat Aspis, even if it killed me.

'Do it! Fucking do it.' I closed my eyes. 'I deserve it.'

When Dad and I finally finished shouting at each other and came back, Mom was sprawled on the rock. Her face was the color of ash. Her eyelids fluttered madly. We got an airlift to the hospital, but it was already too late.

'It was my fault. I did it.'

Mallory had given me a hint, that last night in the Harbour. The DNA template for circular mRNA. I should have seen it then, right away. But I did not want to see.

Mom had been wrong to trust me with the cloning step. Such a simple thing. Add one sequence in the DNA we used to make the RNA circles, to mark the start of the genetic code that Mom's cells needed to read.

I had added two, by accident. Two beginnings made an end. That second starting point produced a partial version of p53 that was even more broken than Mom's own. Our old sequencer must have missed the error. Structured DNA was tricky for nanopores – the same vulnerability the Heffalump had used against my Aspis. I had spent all this time staring at the mRNA and protein, and looking away from the DNA.

Of course I had. Otherwise I might have realized the truth.

A giant sat on my chest. I couldn't breathe.

We waited endless hours and days in the hospital. Dad ate KitKats from the vending machine. I sat on the floor. Finally, they took us to her. I touched her curled-up hand. The skin was cold and dry. I wanted to run away and look for her, anywhere but there. The still wax doll was not her anymore.

'I killed her,' I said. The words barely came out. 'I killed her.'

Far away, someone sobbed and wailed. I touched my face. It was wet, but the sound was not mine. I opened my eyes.

Veil was curled up in her seat, face buried in her hands. She had torn tufts of hair from her head and her scalp was bleeding.

She looked up at me. Her face was a wound of indescribable loss. There were nail marks on cheeks. Running make-up turned her eyes into dark holes. Her mouth gaped open and then she screamed, a shrill, keening sound. She still clutched the gun in one hand, knuckles white, hand shaking, teeth bared in a rictus-like, mirthless grin.

217

I reached out a hand. 'Veil, please, give me the gun, I'm so sorry—'

'SORRY! I'M SORRY! SORRYSORRYSORRYSORRY- SORRY—'

'I'll make it stop, I promise, please, give me my Eyes—'

She froze, looking at me.

'Make it stop,' she repeated. 'Stop.' A sudden relief washed over her face, almost a smile.

And then she shoved the gun's barrel against the bottom of her jaw and pulled the trigger.

23

The Becoming

The report was deafening in the confined space. I collapsed across the seats, holding my ringing ears. Nausea rose into my mouth and I retched, remnants of a long-ago lunch. It forced me to sit up.

I wiped my mouth. Veil was staring at the blood-spattered ceiling above her. No, not Veil any more. I had killed her. I hadn't meant to, but I *had* killed her.

I might as well have pulled the trigger. Again.

The touchscreen came to life. 'A weapon has been fired inside the vehicle,' the car's neutral voice said. 'There appears to be a medical emergency. Authorities are being notified. Rerouting to the nearest medical facility.' The line of our route jumped to Santa Clara Valley Medical Center in San Jose, five miles away. The car picked up its pace. We could get there in ten minutes.

I didn't have the strength to move. OK, I thought. I'm going to lie back. I'll keep my eyes closed. When I open them, there will be nurses and doctors and cops, and I'll tell them everything. Then this will finally be over. The car's interior smelled of blood and my vomit and gunpowder. But

I only needed to stand it for a little while—

The car shuddered. I jerked awake. My battered mind must simply have shut down for a while. Veil was slumped to one side now, what remained of her face thankfully turned away from me. Something was happening on the touchscreen. The car was changing course again, routing back to the road that led to the mountains, but the destination was in the middle of nowhere, close to Mount Umunhum.

My thoughts were slow and heavy and stumbled over each other, but it wasn't hard to figure out what was going on. The car had been hacked and rerouted. Maybe that had been the plan all along, to give Veil deniability; maybe they had access to the car's sensors and knew that something had happened to Veil.

A part of me didn't care anymore. I deserved whatever was going to happen to me. But if Soloviov won, he'd hurt others, too. The thought gave me the strength to pull myself up.

I tapped the touchscreen. 'Restore previous route. Gun fired, remember? Notify authorities. Let's go to the hospital. Right now. Call 911. Call 911!'

Nothing happened. The system was locked. I tried the window controls and the doors. Both were shut tight.

The touchscreen came to life. A video call window opened.

It was Soloviov. His silver eyes had the same intensity as in the Spliceasy, but the smile wasn't there.

'Sereia,' he said. 'Or should I say, Inara.'

I stared. He steepled his fingers. 'I confess I am still trying to understand what happened. What did you do to poor Veil? Such a tragedy. She had so much more to give. Did you know she had a wife and three children?' He shook his head. 'What a waste. Losing a mother. You, better than anyone, should know how that feels.'

I started shaking and closed my eyes. *Shut up shut up shut up*, I thought.

'No matter,' Soloviov said. 'She did her duty admirably. I wanted to let you know that her death does not change the outcome, not in the slightest. It merely adds to your already considerable karmic weight.

'You could have avoided most of it so easily, with a single decision. There is a parallel universe where you chose to work with me twenty-four hours ago. I want you to imagine that world, Inara. A world where you are the hero instead of the villain. Where you are not responsible for a bioterror attack on the Aspis that killed two dozen people, and for shooting Veil Montgomery in the head. Where the only crime you need to redeem yourself for is your mother's murder.'

I made a small, whimpering sound.

'Yes, I heard what you told Veil,' Soloviov said. 'You made a mistake somewhere, didn't you? Such irony. Poor Manuela could have joined PROSPERITY-A if she had lived only a few months longer.' He shook his head again slowly. 'It does make me wonder about the simulation argument.'

I tried to scream, but my vocal cords didn't obey. Desperately, I clawed at his words, looking for any purchase, for a flaw to grasp, to keep me from falling back into the abyss of my guilt.

He spread his hands wide.

'Inara, I want you to know that we are *all* flawed. Your friend Jerome has his own wound, no less terrible than yours. My own hands are stained, with more red than you can possibly imagine.

221

'But there is someone who can forgive you, forgive all of us. Not a god, not some weak, crucified redeemer. I am talking about our future selves, Inara. The luminous beings who sleep within us. And you – you, Inara – you have the power to wake them.'

I wanted to believe him, then. I almost did. Was this what he had offered Veil? Forgiveness for some transgression, a promise of redemption? But that did not exist for me. The only person who could offer it was long gone.

'You don't have to say anything. It has been a hard day, I know. There is a long road ahead. I will help you walk it, if you let me.

'And should you choose a different path this time, too ...'

The smile appeared, the sharp canines, a wolf's smile. 'Well, I think at least a part of you will agree that what happens then is only justice. I am giving you a second chance, Inara. Don't squander it. Now, get some rest. I will see you soon.'

The image blinked out.

I slumped back down in the seat. I floated in a cold, dark ocean. I squeezed my eyes shut but couldn't hold the tears in. 'I'm sorry,' I whispered. 'I'm so sorry.'

Mom had trusted me. *We are a team, peixinha.* I heard her voice say my nickname. And I remembered the fish on the beach, drowning in the sand.

I had been five years old. We found the fish in the tide pool, a tiny thing, barely alive in the stale water heated by the sun. I told Mom I wanted to help it. She nodded and said we'd take it back to the ocean together.

I cupped my hands and she put the fish there with a bit of water. I screamed with joy and ran across the sand towards the waves. I stumbled, and the fish fell. It flapped on the ground and I cried until Mom came and picked it up and put it back in my hands. She held them together with her own for the rest of the way, and as soon as we placed the fish into the ocean, it slipped away, a tiny silver flash in the waves.

'I'm sorry I tripped, Mommy,' I said.

'It's OK,' she said seriously. 'That's why we have two sets of hands.' Then she flashed me a jubilant smile. 'Besides, you tripped in the right direction.'

I had made a mistake. But we *had* been a team. I was *not* supposed to carry the fish alone. Mom had known what she was doing. Maybe I would never forgive myself for the cloning error. But I couldn't let it drown me. Otherwise, Mom would have died for nothing. I would have killed Veil for nothing.

I opened my eyes.

I moved over to the other side of the car, and gingerly searched for my Eyes in Veil's blazer pocket. When my fingers closed around them, the car jumped, and her limply hanging head snapped forward, revealing the gaping hole in the top of her skull. I retched again, but only clear liquid came out. I forced myself to close her eyes, laid her down across her seats and covered her with her blazer. There was a hard cylinder in her other pocket: another Neurocin syringe from the medkit. I took that as well.

Then I put my Eyes on.

For a moment, seeing the open terminal windows and apps felt like coming home. Then the gut-punch of disappointment hit. There was no network connection: we were in the middle of nowhere. The car might have its own satellite connection, but the Eyes didn't. I tried to pair them, but in vain – whoever was in control of the car now had been sure to isolate me completely.

Boxed breathing. In, one, two, three, four. Hold, one, two, three, four. I closed my eyes and kept at it for a minute. Very slowly, my heart rate settled down. I drank from the water bottle Veil had given me, and that helped a little. Trees whizzed past behind the darkened windows. Each flash made me jump. This was no good. I couldn't be scared, weak Inara, the little fish. I had to become something else.

I pulled up my super-soldier serum bookmarks and scanned through the list. I needed something to help me think better, first of all, and then I could prepare for whatever was coming. One command to Donnie gave me a cocktail of neuropeptides: endorphins, orexin, NPY, all with blood-brain barrier crossing motifs. My jailbroken Aspis grew warmer on my arm. They worked much faster than the LuxLives payload. After ten minutes, a feeling of complete calm descended over me.

Everything felt three-dimensional and lucid, as if I was sitting at the bottom of a crystal clear pool of water. I felt the guilt and self-loathing looking at Veil's still body, but the emotions had no grab, no roots. They were simply re-flections among all the others, like my fear, my anger, the sense of being in my body, the seat against my back, the smell of blood and vomit.

It felt natural and safe to gaze into the space around me and ask it a question: what should I do?

I watched the parts of the problem move and dance in the pool of my mind like brightly coloured butterflies. There was a memory from going to San Pablo with Jerome, when he wanted to show off the latest trick he'd come up with. We had spotted a sleek Tesla Pegasus sitting on a lone parking lot. *That would be a cool ride*, I'd said.

Want to take it for a spin?

Don't be ridiculous.

It's easy. Look —

He'd had an aerosol bottle with bits of smallpox genome and skin flakes to mask our own DNA. He made me spray it all over the car, the can hissing in my hand, and I'd laughed out of sheer joy at doing something forbidden. Then the doors unlocked: all Teslas had a biodefence mode that obliged them to offer shelter to anyone during a lockdown. The back doors popped open, and we climbed in. Once we were inside, he showed the interior camera a complex QR code on his flatscreen, and it immediately thought we were its owner—

I pulled back from the memory and the long, sweaty afternoon that had followed. There it was. Soloviov's hackers might have the car under control, but thanks to the Decade, every car had a biodefence mode, baked into the firmware. And given this one was meant to transport Aspis personnel to a safe location, I was betting it was even better equipped with biosensors than the average vehicle. Maybe I could use Jerome's trick and force a factory reset. I had no pre-made DNA spray, of course, but I had something better.

I took Veil's Aspis, gingerly pulling it away from her skin. My calm wavered, but didn't break. Her chip was still talking to my app, so it was easy enough to reprogram it to make a list of RNAs from random Plague viruses — nothing functional, short transcripts, no stealth sequences, something that any sophisticated biosensor system would immediately recognise.

In a few minutes, tiny droplets of RNA beaded in the microneedles at the Aspis's bottom, and very carefully I held it over a ventilation intake and shook it until a few fell in. I repeated the exercise in a couple of different spots. If Soloviov's goons were watching, they might realise something was up, but I didn't care.

Nothing happened for a couple of minutes. Then the touchscreen flickered and the frozen map was replaced with an entirely new menu. The car app showed up in my glasses now – I was sure that previously it would only have been accessible to Aspis personnel, but obviously the biodefence mode meant that someone else might have to use the vehicle in an emergency.

The normal me would have whooped, but Inara in super-soldier mode saw the delight pop up in my chest like a colourful bubble, and dissipate, transient and insubstantial.

I opened the car app. Satellite connection – there. My Eyes pinged with incoming messages: it seemed the network block on my communication apps had been local to the Spire. I was hungry for news, but first things first. I reset the car's destination and increased the speed to the maximum allowed. That actually worried me – if Soloviov's lackeys came after me, I very much doubted they would stick to speed limits. But at least it would buy me some time.

Then I told Donnie to reap the news whirlwind. I wanted to know what had happened in the Spire after I left – and if there was any substance to Soloviov's claims that I would get the blame.

The story of the attack on Aspis had broken, and it was big. My Eyes exploded with headlines, summarised articles and video clips.

Wall Street in Panic as Aspis HQ is Attacked with Suspected Bioweapon.

Eyes footage, jerking and wobbling. A man beating on a co-worker, another chewing on his own arm.

Aspis Attack Super-Virus: Can it Be Stopped?

A mass of flashing red and blue lights around the Aspis campus, emergency services attempting to secure a perimeter. Crowd control barriers thrown askew, a mass of people rushing past them.

Aspis's 9/11: This is Why We Need the Zephyra Lux Act.

Drone footage of the Spire. Plumes of dark smoke pouring out. A lone human figure, falling.

Another Decade of Plagues: Are our Aspises Now Useless?

A clip of Amanda Shah played next to practically every headline. I eyeclicked it.

Shah stood against a white backdrop with the Aspis logo. She looked exhausted but composed. Seeing her felt surreal: had I really argued with her just hours ago?

She locked her unwavering gaze on the camera.

'As you know by now, the Aspis headquarters has been targeted with a bioweapon in a premeditated terror attack,' she said. 'First and foremost, let me assure you that the Aspis biodefence network remains fully operational, and is performing exactly as it was designed to do. The weapon has been identified and contained. We have rolled out a patch to over three billion Aspis devices to deliver a pre-emptive countermeasure. We are in active collaboration with local, national, and global authorities to protect public health.

'However, I am heartbroken to report that at last count, twenty-seven Aspis employees have lost their lives. Our thoughts are with their families and loved ones. Many more remain affected. We will move mountains to ensure they receive the best possible care.'

Shah paused and closed her eyes for a second. When she opened them, her gaze was steely.

'This is more than an attack on Aspis,' she said. 'It's an affront to everything Aspis stands for: compassion, healing and freedom from fear.

'To all of you who rely on us for their health and safety, and the health and safety of their children: we will not let you down. This malicious act is a brazen attempt to shatter our trust in each other and to delay the launch of our Panacea platform, set to transform healthcare. Let us stand together in the face of this tragedy. I only ask you this: misinformation can be as deadly as the enemy we face – verify before sharing.

'And to the planners and perpetrators of today's evil, I say only this. You have summoned a storm. You will find no shelter anywhere on this planet.'

She turned on her heels and walked offscreen, leaving the Aspis logo blinking behind her.

I swallowed. So much for trying to contact Aspis for help. If Repo was still alive, what he would put together was exactly the scenario Soloviov had described. I had been the Zemyevit Disease vector. I had pretended to hand myself in to Aspis to get access to their facilities to complete the jailbreak. Then I had killed Veil on the way to the Arc and escaped. From what Soloviov had said, he'd have doctored any recordings in the hacked car to make it look exactly like that.

And if someone as high up as Veil had been working for Soloviov, it was doubtful that she was the only Aspis mole.

I opened the Darkome app. There was a flood of *aspis-offleash* notifications and forum chatter on the Aspis attack, but I ignored them and scanned down the seemingly endless list. *There.* A message from Holst.

> Message received, it said. > If you want to follow us, remember the mycelium.

A bubble of relief and joy floated through the crystal sphere of my mind. I held on to it for a moment before letting it go. Then I turned to the regular messages.

There were several from Svetlana. I swallowed and deleted them without reading them: I couldn't resist responding if I did, and it was better if she wasn't drawn any closer to my orbit. I didn't think Soloviov knew about our friendship, and it was better to keep it that way – with no electronic trail if I was captured and my Eyes were compromised.

If I wanted to stay ahead of Soloviov, I needed to act fast. That meant doing things I had been putting off for too long.

I took a deep breath and BodyTimed Dad.

He answered almost immediately, AI-generated 3D image in my Eyes neatly positioned across from me, sitting naturally, regardless of what he was actually doing. I made sure to completely blur my surroundings, and tidied up my own features – I didn't want him seeing Veil's corpse, or what a mess I was.

'Peixinha,' he said. 'I was starting to get worried.'

I said nothing and looked at him, the distorted reflection of my own face but without the genetic taint of Li-Fraumeni. With super-soldier clarity, I could see the concern and the kindness on it, the lines of worry and fear.

'It ... sounds like I should be worried,' he said. 'Is that right?'

'Yes,' I said. 'Dad ... I'm sorry. I have been very angry at you for a long time, and a part of me still is, but I am sorry about last time. It wasn't fair.'

'OK,' he said. 'I appreciate that. Why do I sense a but coming?'

'Because ...' I swallowed. 'You ... you saved me. I didn't want you to, but you did. You couldn't protect Mom, but you found a way to protect me, and you did it, even if it was against my will. Even if it meant leaving my old life behind, forcing me to become someone else.'

'Inara,' he said. 'I'm sorry. I know I did, and I wish there was a way I could tell you that I wouldn't do it again, but—'

'It's OK,' I said. 'I understand.' There was a lump in my throat now. 'I finally do. Because ... I'm so sorry, Dad, but I'm going to have to do the same to you.'

His eyes widened. 'What do you mean?'

'I need you to leave everything, Dad,' I said. 'Right now. I can't explain it, but there are some very bad people who will come after you to get to me. You might have a couple of hours, and that's it. I'm sending you a Darkome how-to on how to jailbreak your Eyes and go dark. Leave work. Don't go home. Do everything the how-to says and get to where we had the last Brazilian night. Can you do that for me? Right now? Can you trust me? There is no time to explain.'

'Inara, I'm not sure that I can—'

'It's not fair, Dad, I know. Believe me, this is not me taking revenge on you. I *want* you to be happy, and this is the last thing I want to do to you. But if you love me, if you loved Mom, you will do this. If you want to protect me, you *will* do this. Because you are the sail and the anchor, and I need you to stay alive.'

He folded both hands as if in prayer, and pressed them against his mouth.

'You sound just like her,' he whispered.

'That's because I'm the captain now,' I said. And for the first time, I understood what it truly meant, and how much I wished that I wasn't.

The rearview mirror screen in the car app highlighted movement, suddenly, a car in the distance, a large SUV, gaining fast. I had to get ready.

'I need to go, Dad,' I said. 'I love you. I'll see you soon, OK?'

'OK,' he said. 'I love you too, peixinha. Sail safe.'

The image winked out. I took Veil's gun and checked it. It was exactly the kind of weapon Repo would carry: nothing digital, no biometric security even, no HUD, advanced stealth materials and solid design, 5.5mm ammunition, ten bullets left. I wasn't a great shot, but Juniper in the Harbour had been into guns, and she had shown me the basics. I had shot at a few cardboard targets in the Naval Depot.

The car in the rearview mirror approached. It was dark on the road in the mountains, and all I could see were the headlights, like the eyes of a great beast against the black. It was gaining more slowly now as the road got more curvy. I had maybe fifteen minutes.

There was no way out. The people coming after me would be the most vocal, most extreme fans of DzoGene on Darkome – all about self-enhancement. They wouldn't have Aspises, and they would have dosed themselves with mRNA or AAV gene therapies that made them feel like badasses, maybe for years, to enhance muscle growth, cognition, reflexes. Four or five of them. Armed.

231

I had never been in a real fight. I had no idea how to fight. I didn't even know how to drive. They would force me off the road, or ram the car. The self-drive would be conservative and stop: I couldn't force it into crazy manoeuvres. If what Veil had said was true, they wouldn't hesitate to kill. They just needed enough of the Heffalump to make a tumour organoid system. My guts were a tense coil of steel rope, even through the neuropeptide-induced calm.

But death was something I had already accepted when I saw the Heffalump's highways under my skin. It held no fear for me. And every animal knew how to fight. Even Clementine, sweet, floppy-eared Clementine, had ancient instincts from wolves and had bared her teeth when cornered.

If there was one thing I had learned from Soloviov, it was never to play the game you were offered. I needed to become the hunter. But becoming would take time, and I didn't have long.

I stuck Veil's Aspis on my right thigh, in the muscle, well away from the osteosarcoma scar. That doubled the mRNA delivery capacity and reagents. I dumped the rest of the super-soldier folder sequences into my system. Adrenergic receptors and adenylyl cyclase to boost the effects of adrenaline, PKA and PhK for short term strength boosts, new $Ca2+$ channels. Dopamine receptors and NT-3 for enhanced cognition. I hesitated for a moment before adding a modified rhodopsin channel for night vision and pressing the microneedles of my own Aspis against my right eyeball like a torturer's contact lens. It stung a bit, but it was the fastest way to get the mRNA directly where it needed to go.

By the time I was done, the two Aspises were burning on my skin like cigarette stubs. I was sweating, heart hammering, temples pounding, and I felt a fever coming on. I would pay for dumping so much mRNA into my body at once, despite any fancy chemistry to make it invisible to the immune system. The water of the crystal pool of my mind was churning and bubbling. Maybe this had been a mistake, and I would end up like Zephyra Lux, killed by an autoimmune reaction. Soloviov would appreciate the irony.

My eyes felt warm, and teared up. I blinked and suddenly the dim light of the touchscreen was unbearably bright. It was time.

I told the car to slow down to ten miles per hour for ten seconds, and then to accelerate back to maximum speed limit. The roadside had a shallow dirt ditch that looked soft in my new night-adapting eyes. I opened the door, tucked my chin against my chest, shielded my face with my arms and rolled out. I landed on grassy ground that absorbed some of the impact, but it still felt like a whole-body punch. I lay still for a minute.

The pursuers' car sped past. Nothing seemed broken, although my shoulder hurt. Through my endorphin cloud, it was distant and abstract, barely a damage report. I got up and started running.

24

The Hunter

The forest road was narrow and winding. There were tall trees on the right side, and a steep slope on the left. It smelled of rotting leaves and damp soil.

I breathed more easily in the cool air. I kept to the roadside as I ran, following the receding lights of the cars ahead. They flickered through the gaps between the trees. The owl-like rhodopsins gave the night strange, shifting colours. There were blurry patches in my vision, but a sliver of a moon was up, and I could see almost as well as in daylight.

Then one set of lights stopped moving and went out. They had forced the Aspis car off the road, maybe half a mile ahead. I accelerated, my stride lengthening, breath quickening. The adrenaline thrummed in my temples as my momentum built. A rocky outcrop jutted from the hillside ahead, and I scrambled up it, barely slowing down, to get a better vantage point.

There was a bend in the road ahead. The Aspis vehicle was angled awkwardly and its left tyres were inches from a ditch. Its emergency lights blinked. The pursuing SUV was parked a few hundred feet further along. Three human figures were cautiously proceeding along the road towards my car. It was hard to make out all the details at this distance, but at least two of them were holding weapons. One was bigger than the other two. All were wearing Darkome excursion suits. One more enemy stood next to their vehicle further back, covering the advance of the others.

I took a deep breath. I had to think of them as *zmeyove*, dragons in disguise, not humans: they were enemies, and they wanted to hurt me. I had to hit at the weakest link, fast and hard.

I came down the outcrop carefully on the forest side, and ran towards the SUV, keeping to the cover of the trees. The undergrowth made it difficult but I had done enough trail running with dogs to jump over logs and roots. I was making noise, and, briefly, a flashlight beam shone through the trees. I dived down, and soon the three Soloviov operatives were focused on the Aspis car again.

I came out of the woods behind the SUV. The remaining *zmey* had their back towards me. I took the stopper off the Neurocin injector and approached, step by step.

A branch cracked beneath my trainers. The zmey started to turn round. Without thinking, I leaped forward. I barely had a chance to register what she looked like – tall, wiry woman with braided hair, excursion suit covered in living moss and ivy – before I slammed into her. We both smashed against the side of the car. I kneed her in the stomach as hard as I could. She doubled up. I took hold of her weapon, a short-barrelled automatic rifle, and tore it from her grasp. To my shock, it felt like wrestling a toddler. I threw the rifle into the darkness behind me. The *zmey* straightened up, fists in a fighting stance.

'It's Reyes!' she screamed and lunged at me, but she was moving in slow motion. I sidestepped, did a poor imitation of Repo's choke hold, and stabbed her in the side of her neck with the Neurocin.

She fell to the ground almost instantly. There was no need to be quiet any more. Running footsteps and flickering flashlight beams approached down the road. I put a round into each of the SUV's tyres. I didn't think I could pull off another carjacking, but at least I could make pursuit harder. Then I ran back into the woods, deeper this time, and doubled back towards the Aspis car. Retaking it was my best chance to get away.

My heart hammered in my chest. Boosted adrenaline response or not, I could not keep this up for very long.

As I got closer, I crawled through the undergrowth and hid behind a fallen log. The doors of the Aspis car, fifty feet ahead, were open. Veil's body had been pulled out and lay on the ground. I had hoped to draw all the *zmeyove* away from the vehicle, but no such luck – one had stayed behind, a tall wiry figure in a dark excursion suit, scanning the trees with a flashlight, a weapon ready. There would be no surprise attack this time: if I wanted to get out of here, I would have to shoot them from cover.

Gritting my teeth, I took aim at their centre of mass – and recognised the excursion suit.

It was Jerome.

A thousand thoughts flashed through my head. Had he lied to me about helping me? He had to have known about the Zemyevit attack on the Spire. Or maybe he had kept his word, trying to buy me time, and as soon as I had turned myself in to Repo, Veil had reported back to Soloviov, and Jerome had nothing to do with it.

It didn't matter. He was in my way, but I could not shoot him in cold blood.

I took aim, kept a bead on him, and came out of the woods slowly and carefully.

'Jerome,' I said. 'Not a word, or I will shoot.'

He froze and turned slowly around, hands up. In my night vision, his face was pale as a vampire's. Very slowly, he nodded.

I came up close, barely out of arm's reach, gun pointed at his face. I tried to make my face look cold, imagined the dragon behind his green eyes. 'Weapon to the ground. Give me your Eyes and earpiece,' I said, 'slowly.'

Very carefully, he did as he was told. I pocketed the Eyes and the earpod with one hand, keeping the weapon trained on him. From the corner of my eye, I saw movement close to the SUV. I didn't have much time.

'Inara,' Jerome said. 'I'm so glad you're OK.'

'What the hell are you doing here?'

Reflected movement flickered in his green eyes.

Oh. You're bait, I thought.

Someone lunged from behind the car and tackled me with the force of a train.

At first I thought it was a bear, but it was the large *zmey*. His excursion suit had fake fur and claws, making him look even bigger. His weight crushed me down and the back of my head hit the asphalt. Black stars sparked in my eyes. His respirator was contoured and meshed to accommodate a massive, braided beard that reached down to his chest and smelled of some pungent oil. He held my gun hand down with a huge glove with claws, and punched me in the face with the other. I managed to turn my head in time. The blow glanced off my cheek, but I still felt the disgusting crack of bone on bone. The claws bit into my wrist. The pain was a distant damage report, but I couldn't stop my fingers from letting go of the gun.

'Let her go!' Jerome shouted. That helped. The same rage I had felt in Point Molate exploded in me like a volcano. I grabbed the man's beard braids with my left hand, pulled on them as hard as I could, and head-butted him in the nose at the same time. It crunched like a giant shrimp between teeth.

The man roared, clutching his face. I kept my hold on the beard braids and wrenched them to one side with all my strength. Some tore loose with a ripping sound, but the man toppled off me. I rolled away, picked up the gun and put six bullets in his chest. It was only when the hammer clicked on an empty chamber that I realised I was screaming.

My breath ran out before the scream did, and then I stood there, gasping. Suddenly, the gun weighed a ton, so I let it fall to the ground. Everything felt heavy. My endorphins fought a losing battle against a piercing needle of pain in my cheekbone and a dull ache across the entire left side of my ribcage. My knees gave in and I toppled forward.

Jerome caught me. He pulled my arm around his shoulders and half-walked, half-carried me towards the car.

'So, this is it?' I muttered in a daze. I had no strength to fight any more. 'Catching me so your boss can harvest my tumour for world domination? I guess that finally counts as a break-up.'

He shoved me in the seat and looked at me. 'Stay here and

be quiet,' he said. 'Wait five minutes, then go. There's only Shadow left, and I'll lead her away.' He held out a hand. 'I need the pod and the Eyes back.'

I looked at him. In the dark, the golden flecks in his eyes were like tiny stars.

I nodded and handed him the earpiece and the glasses.

'I'll find a way to help you,' I whispered. 'I'll set you free. I promise.'

He grinned, like the day we had met, when I had caught him breaking into Darin's ice cream truck.

'You already have,' he said. 'Goodbye, Inara.' Then he slipped the earpiece into his ear and put the Eyes on.

'Shadow! She got Marcus!' he shouted. 'She's in the woods, I'm in pursuit! Follow my marker!'

He broke into a run and fired into the trees. With my night eyes I watched him go deeper into the forest. Briefly, his silhouette was illuminated by a muzzle flash, and then he was gone.

Hand on my chest, next to the Heffalump, I counted five hundred heartbeats, and started the long drive home.

25

The Harbour

And so it was that I finally came back to the Harbour, in the back of a self-drive that smelled of blood and vomit, alone and in pain. I had spent the last of my Aspis reagent cassettes on a burst of anti-pain monoclonals, so it was bearable, but only in the way that squeezing a broken glass in your hand is bearable.

It was four in the morning when I arrived. There was the faintest touch of blue in the sky. The car came down the last descent to the Harbour, down the hillside road lined with gnarly brambles. I passed the ancient twin rail tracks, and then the horseshoe formed by the beach and the wavebreaker came into view.

All the houseboats were gone. The piers were empty. The few structures on solid ground like the Dark Star BBQ and the goat shed were empty and dark. The only light sources were the faint bioluminescence of the giant bee, and the new sculpture at the end of the wavebreaker — like an inverted tree, a white profusion of tendrils in the shape of a mushroom, reaching in all directions. I didn't need many guesses as to what it represented and who had made it. Both structures glowed with the faintest hint of blue I might not even have been able to see without my night vision.

The one sign of life was an old-fashioned car sitting close to the giant gramophone statue. Dad's ancient Dodge Charger. Cool, soothing relief flooded my chest.

The darksense buzzed on my wrist: it felt like a hand-shake from an old friend. *Remember the mycelium,* Holst's message had said, and I thought I knew what it meant. It was dangerous to be here, I knew. But I trusted Holst and Mallory to have laid false trails for us, and between the ongoing chaos at the Spire and whatever sacrifice Jerome had made, we should have a couple of hours, more than we needed.

I told the car to stop close to Dad's. He was huddling by the gramophone, wearing a thick puffy jacket.

'Hi, peixinha,' he said, when I got out. 'It's a cold night out here.'

'You came,' I said, and hugged him.

'That's a good grip you have,' he breathed, but hugged back. I flinched when my ribs lit up again. He noticed and pushed me away.

'Oh my God. Your face. What happened to you?'

'It's a long story,' I said. 'I need to pick up something for us here, and then we can go. We don't have a lot of time.'

Face full of concern, he nodded. Then he sighed. 'Inara, I have to tell you something. I didn't come alone.'

Sudden fear of a betrayal lanced through my heart. I looked around for flashlights, for police with guns, for more of Dimitry's operatives. And then a small woman stepped from the gramophone's shadow, and put her hand on Dad's arm.

241

'This is Kamala,' Dad said sheepishly. 'She insisted on coming along.'

The woman looked at me, frowning, then attempted a smile. She was petite, with warm eyes and streaks of silver in her dark hair.

'Hi, Inara. I ... was looking forward to meeting you, but not quite like this.' She had a soft lilting accent.

I stared at her.

'Yeah. Hi.' I looked at Dad. 'This will be dangerous, right? I don't know where we are going. Some really scary people might come after us. And ... and there will probably be some news about me, claiming I did things I didn't do. Are you sure you want her to be a part of that?'

'It's not up to me,' he said quietly. 'In the past, I have tried to make decisions for other people, and that didn't work out well.'

I turned back to Kamala. 'It's not too late to go home. You don't know me. You don't owe me anything. It's not fair for me to ask you to do this.'

'Inara, *you* are not asking. I am asking,' she said. 'Your father is the kindest, most honest person I have ever met. He is incapable of lying. If he says you are innocent of whatever you are accused of, I believe him. And if you are going to do something dangerous, I want to help.'

'But ... your work, the Mojave Project, it – it's too much—'

'It will go on,' she said. 'It doesn't need us. But I'm thinking you do.'

She looked around. 'David told me what happened here, to your mother. I can only imagine what it means to you for him to be with someone else. But that is life. We hurt. We heal. We evolve.'

'We become,' I said.

Kamala nodded. 'I look forward to getting to know you, Inara. Whoever you are and will be.'

I thought about what the old me would have said, the one weighed down by oncosense. She would have wanted to punish Dad, have him lose everything as completely as I had, to send Kamala home. But that wasn't necessary.

And, if he and Kamala were stronger together, we'd all need that strength in the days and months ahead.

'Me too,' I said. 'Thank you.'

Then I gave in to the insistent buzzing of the darksense, and motioned them to follow.

It led us to the mycelium sculpture, to the faintly glowing tracery of lines that seemed to connect the few remaining stars in the pre-dawn sky. I found the spot where the sense was the warmest, a barely visible dot on the structure's white plaster trunk, a bird dropping or a rainwater stain.

I put on my Eyes, took off my Aspis and gently rubbed its microneedle surface on the mark. The chip's nanopore lit up with sequences. I fed them into the Darkome app, expecting an encoded message or a darksense location. But the data kept coming, more and more of it, a full Darkome snapshot, updating the app itself, rewriting it –

When it was done, it looked completely different. No more reagent markets, project repos, genetic libraries or forums. Just a new layer, superimposed on the world. And a line of light, snaking along the ground, gently glowing.

We followed it to the beach and along the shoreline. The darksense had changed, too: it whispered as long as I stayed on the line, more subtle than before. I looked back at Kamala and Dad. They followed me, hand in hand.

243

There was so much they still didn't know, about the Heffalump, about Soloviov. I had to protect them. And the only way to do it was to get rid of the Heffalump once and for all. Soloviov would never stop coming until the thing he wanted was gone.

I hesitated for a moment. If I followed the trail into this new Darkome labyrinth, I would be putting Mallory and Holst and the others in danger, too. They had already taken a huge risk by helping. But I had a jailbroken Aspis: maybe I could help them and Darkome in turn. And I trusted Holst. What was it that he had said to me in the Dark Star, that night?

Maybe you are the virus that lets us be born.

I had no idea what he meant, but I was going to find out.

It would be the fight of my life, but I wasn't alone. Maybe, just maybe, I even had a family again.

The darksense took us to the waterline, among rocks, and then it continued into the waters of the Bay. In the distance, fog was starting to roll down the hills, obscuring the city from view. But within it, more Darkome lines glowed, threads of information, guiding, connecting.

Hidden behind a large rock was a small boat, a sleek thing painted light blue and white, with a solid engine and a low mast. It bobbed gently in the waves. I climbed in. Inside was a large plastic crate that lit up blue when I looked at it. It had a biometric reader. I touched it and it opened.

It contained a small but complete molecular biology kit, three pairs of burner Eyes, three new passports and two drivers' licences. I leafed through them. It looked like I was now Maya Singh, and Dad and Kamala were James and Priya Lee, a married couple.

I remembered what Jerome had said about Holst launching a backup identity programme. I looked at Dad, frowning. 'I told Holst I had to go into hiding only days ago. How did he—'

Dad shrugged. 'He checked up on me about a month ago,' he said. 'I told him about Kamala. I'm guessing he wanted to cover all the bases.'

I nodded – near-supernatural foresight was on brand for Holst.

'Last chance to get off the boat,' I told Kamala. She hesitated, looking at her face in the passport with the wrong name. Then she closed it.

'It's not every day you get married,' she said. 'I always wanted to elope.' She smiled a little wistfully. 'When wishes come true, it's often not how we imagined them.'

I gave the quiet, silent Harbour one last look, and nodded.

While Dad untied the rope from an iron ring in a rock, Kamala sat down at the helm.

'So, where are we going?' she asked.

The blue line of the new mycelium snaked across the water.

'To the new lands, beyond the sea,' I said.

Dad sat down next to me and put his arm across my shoulders. The electric motor hummed to life. The boat leaped forward across the waves, chasing Darkome's trail.

TO BE CONTINUED

Acknowledgements

This was the toughest book I have written so far, and the most personal. Fortunately, I had more help than ever before. The origin story of *Darkome* is convoluted and so entwined with my life that I wrote a separate essay on it you can read online[1]. These pages are simply for gratitude, for the mycelium of minds that helped this book grow.

First, there are the books. Marcus Wohlsen's *Biopunk* was my first deep dive into the world of garage biology. I learned the basics of molecular biology from Bruce Alberts' classic textbook *Molecular Biology of the Cell*, and immunology from Lauren Sompayrac's supremely accessible *How the Immune System Works*. There is perhaps no greater contemporary expositor of the wonders and horrors of biology and medicine than Siddartha Mukherjee. *The Emperor of All Maladies*, *The Gene* and *The Song of the Cell* are among the best books I have read in any genre. I recommend all of the above to anyone who wants to learn more about how our cells and bodies work.

And then the friends, colleagues, supporters and beta readers: I am grateful to Joshua Achiam, David Eagleman for neosenses, Esa Hilli, Katan'Hya, Michael Kleinman, Fawaz

1 https://bit.ly/4eMPree

Al-Matrouk, Michael Nielsen, Ramez Naam, Brian Pascal, Eliot Peper, Lenny Raymond, Cooper Rinzler, Kim Stanley Robinson for wise words, Arnav Shah, Peter Schwartz, Robin Sloan, Hal Stern and Jo Zayner for their many comments, excellent suggestions and inspiration.

David Kong introduced me to the world of community biology and continues to build a much less dark Darkome in real life, for hundreds of students worldwide. Thank you for showing us what's possible.

My co-founder Nikolai Eroshenko taught me how to think about experiments, evolution and startups, and designed the perfect writing schedule -compatible weightlifting program. Julia Carvalho embodies my faith in humanity and helped dispel limiting beliefs. The rest of the HelixNano team keeps demonstrating how to build the best parts of a biological future together: thank you, all.

My past readers and the Gollancz team, Marcus and John: you have been more patient and understanding than I deserve. I hope the wait was worth it.

Dustin DiPerna, Ben Tauber and Victoria Song helped me get out of my own way, refine my mission and discover new modes of being.

My father Mauno Rajaniemi showed me how to never give up on something you love, and my son Kasper continues to teach me how to be a father.

Finally, my wind and sail throughout this journey was my wife Zuzana, who knows how to care for all living things, from brain organoids to stressed writers. I would be lost without her wisdom. Our second child will be born soon after this book is published, a miracle of cells and DNA, a shared becoming.

Credits

Hannu Rajaniemi and Gollancz would like to thank everyone at Orion who worked on the publication of *Darkome* in the UK.

Editor
Marcus Gipps
Zakirah Alam

Copyeditor
Elizabeth Dobson

Proofreader
Andy Ryan

Audio
Paul Stark

Editorial Management
Charlie Panayiotou
Jane Hughes

Design
Nick Shah
Rachael Lancaster
Joanna Ridley

Contracts
Dan Herron

Finance
Nick Gibson
Jasdip Nandra
Sue Baker

Marketing
Hennah Sandhu